# A Dark Touch Novel
# FEVER

## Amy Meredith

**RED FOX**

DARK TOUCH: FEVER
A RED FOX BOOK 978 1 849 41147 9

First published in Great Britain by Red Fox,
an imprint of Random House Children's Books
A Random House Group Company

This edition published 2011

1 3 5 7 9 10 8 6 4 2

Series created and developed by Amber Caravéo

The Random House Group Limited supports the Forest Stewardship Council
(FSC), the leading international forest certification organization. All our
titles that are printed on Greenpeace-approved FSC-certified paper
carry the FSC logo. Our paper procurement policy can be found at
www.rbooks.co.uk/environment.

**Mixed Sources**
Product group from well-managed
forests and other controlled sources
www.fsc.org   Cert no. TT-COC-2139
© 1996 Forest Stewardship Council

Set in 12.25/16pt Minion by Falcon Oast Graphic Art Ltd.

Red Fox Books are published by Random House Children's Books,
61–63 Uxbridge Road, London W5 5SA

www.kidsatrandomhouse.co.uk
www.rbooks.co.uk

Addresses for companies within The Random House Group Limited can be
found at: www.randomhouse.co.uk/offices.htm

THE RANDOM HOUSE GROUP Limited Reg. No. 954009

A CIP catalogue record for this book is available from the British Library.

Printed and bound in Great Britain by
CPI Bookmarque, Croydon, CRO 4TD

For Shirley Kwan, always an inspiration

# Prologue

Cam Dokey sucked on a stick of hollow white candy that tasted of cinnamon as he wandered through the Souk Gomma – the Friday market in Cairo's City of the Dead. This is what he'd dreamed of when he majored in history at Boston University – trips to exotic lands, learning about other cultures, seeing, smelling, tasting *everything*.

Instead he'd ended up a teacher at Deepdene High in the Hamptons. A good job, a job he enjoyed, but not exactly exotic. *This* was exotic. Every stall in the twisted maze of narrow streets had something different. Over there, mounds of richly coloured spices; and there a squirming mass of snakes being poked at by screaming, laughing children.

Cam tried to remember every detail to tell his students. He allowed himself a smile as he imagined how they'd feel if the boutiques of Main Street were situated in an ancient cemetery, and they occasionally had to skirt around a grave as they shopped. He'd have to tell the kids in his classes that by the end of a day of bargain-hunting in the souk, they'd be covered with fine, grey cemetery dust.

*Thunk!*

He turned towards the sound just in time to see a rabbit hurl itself off the killing table. A woman holding a cleaver yelled after it. She'd never catch it now, even though she'd managed to cut off one of its feet.

Cam tracked the rabbit for a moment as it streaked through the horde of people, trailing droplets of blood. It was heading towards an alley he hadn't explored yet, one that was deep in the shadows of the freeway overpass. Intrigued, Cam headed over, elbows out to help him fight his way through the crowd.

It wasn't just darker in the alley, it was colder too – cold enough to make Cam shiver. He passed by a couple of tables selling old electronic odds and ends that probably didn't work, then reached a mound of clothes at least four metres high. He'd heard rumours that many items of clothing sold in the souk came directly from the bodies of the deceased. The odour – a mix of rot, sweat, urine, sickness and blood – made him believe that the rumours were true.

He started to turn round, but something on the edge of one table on the other side of the towering mountain of clothes caught his eye. As he moved towards it, gooseflesh broke out all over his body. Was he getting a bug? It couldn't be cold enough to cause that reaction. Yes, he was in the shade, but in the shade on a scorching day in Egypt.

He approached the table cautiously. It was covered with odds and ends – old coins, dead cellphones, tattered American magazines from the year before, some empty travel-sized shampoo bottles. Nothing of interest. Cam went to turn away, and then noticed a battered cardboard box near the phones. *Once you see a box, you have to open it, don't you?* he thought.

He opened the flaps, unsure of what he expected to find. Inside he saw a ceramic bowl, almost perfectly round, with a lid. The only decorative element was a row of geometric shapes around the top.

But something about it – something other than its rather plain appearance – seemed to call to him. He gently slid his hands around it. The sensation was like touching dry ice – a coldness so severe it almost burned. What could be producing that kind of chill? He lifted the bowl out of the box and moved one hand up to the lid. Before he could lift it off, an old man, bent double, with skin that looked like leather stretched over bone, scrambled out from behind the tower of clothing and tried to snatch the bowl away.

Instinctively, Cam pulled it tightly against his chest, the bowl's coldness seeping deep into his body, slowing the beat of his heart. 'How much?' he asked the teenager behind the table.

'Ten LE,' the boy shouted. 'Nothing more than ten LE.' About a dollar seventy-five. Cam slapped down a twenty-pound note, twisting his body to keep the bowl away from the old man. He didn't wait for the change.

He started back the way he came, the scent of rot from the tower of clothing suddenly overwhelming. But the old man managed to scuttle in front of him. He spat out a stream of words, his eyes bulging, a few flecks of foam on his lips. He grabbed at the bowl, his long fingernails scraping against the ceramic sides.

'It's mine!' Cam yelled fiercely, a flood of protectiveness and anger surging through him. He pulled out another twenty-pound note and flung it to the ground. 'There, buy yourself two bowls.'

The old man was knocked to the ground as four or five others lunged for the money. Cam used the moment to make his escape. When he had almost reached the mouth of the alleyway, someone grabbed his arm.

Cam, sure it was the old man again, jerked his arm free, then saw it was a little girl who had grabbed his sleeve. 'He said: "Don't open," ' the girl told him. 'He said it will get out. The evil will get out.'

*This will be a great story to tell the kids when I bring the bowl to class,* he thought. *They'll love it.*

# Chapter One

'You'll never believe this. Shanna's got it now!' Eve
Evergold cried. She put her iPhone down on the patio
table next to her sweating glass of mango iced tea. Eve
couldn't blame the glass for sweating – it was only the
first week in March, but the extremely freaky heat
wave made it feel like August.

'Are you kidding?' Jess Meredith, Eve's BFSPF – Best
Friend Since Practically Forever – sat up on her
lounger and pushed her D&G sunglasses onto the top
of her head. The tortoiseshell frames set off her sun-
highlighted blonde hair perfectly. 'How can that be?
Shanna seemed completely OK at school today.'

'I know. But it seems like that's the way it happens.
One second you're fine, the next you feel like you're
about to die.' A shiver ran through Eve despite the
insane heat. Everyone seemed to be getting sick. Flu
X, people were calling it. It wasn't swine flu or bird

flu, although some of the symptoms, like fever and chills and vomiting, were the same. It was a strain no one had ever seen before. Some of the talking heads on TV were saying it wasn't the flu at all. All anybody knew for sure was that it was contagious. Extremely.

'Evie . . .' Jess hesitated. 'I'm scared. I mean, I'm sitting here poolside on a freakishly beautiful day, drinking mangolicious iced tea. But I'm only pretending . . . I don't know *what* I'm pretending.'

'That life is still normal,' Eve answered. 'I'm pretending it too. Or trying. It's like I have the outside down – bikini, lounger, stack of fresh magazines – but on the inside, all I can think about is everyone who's sick.'

'And who will be next,' Jess added.

Eve nodded. 'On the news last night, it said there were about seventy-five cases. But one of them was Charlie Zooper. Do you think he counts as two?' Charlie Zooper was one of the sprinkling of celebs who lived in Deepdene, along with the insanely wealthy people and just your basic very-wealthies.

'No . . . he's not famous enough,' Jess decided. 'Directors are hardly ever famous enough to count as two. Only, like, James Cameron. Or Spielberg, but he lives three towns away, and there aren't any cases of Flu X in East Hampton yet.'

So far the outbreak hadn't moved beyond their little beachside town on Long Island – at least not yet. And, thankfully, not to New York City either, a hundred miles away. Eve didn't even want to think about the disease running through a city that size. She did some calculations in her head. 'If seventy-five people are sick, it means about two thousand people are still healthy,' she said, trying to comfort her friend – and herself. 'That's a lot.'

Eve pressed her cold glass against her forehead, hoping it would cool her down and maybe also stop her brain from racing. She caught Jess staring at her. 'What?'

'Are you OK? Does your forehead feel hot?' Jess asked, her voice tight with concern.

'I don't have a fever.' At least Eve was almost positive she didn't. Could it be the start of one? She shoved the thought away. 'It's just really hot out here.'

'So hot. Like the hottest it's ever been in March,' Jess agreed.

Eve took the bottle of sunscreen off the little table, squirted some into her palm, and smoothed it over her hands and arms.

'Do some hair milk too,' Jess advised.

Eve nodded. She loved her long, dark ringlets, but in weather like this, her hair would never cooperate. It frizzed – with a capital F. It got almost as bad as when she used the powers she'd inherited as a descendant of the Deepdene Witch. She zapped lightning out of her fingers, and – *poof!* – frizz. Eve estimated that she'd doubled her consumption of leave-in conditioner since her powers had started expressing themselves at the beginning of the school year. But some hair issues weren't such a huge price to pay for the ability to destroy demons, especially since Deepdene had turned out to have a door to hell right at its centre.

'I can't believe we're starting to get tan already,' Jess commented. The heatwave had been going on almost as long as the Flu X outbreak, and Eve and Jess had been taking full advantage of the sunshine. Every day, as soon as school finished, they rushed to Eve's, got into their bikinis, and then into the pool in her back yard.

'I know. We've almost reached the point of golden-brown perfection.' Of course, part of it was bronzer. Eve and Jess didn't want to end up with leather skin when they were old. When they were old. That would happen, right? Unless . . .

*Don't go there*, Eve ordered herself. *Focus on the gorgeous, gorgeous, gorgeous weather.* It wasn't as if she could do anything about the disease. She'd saved her town from a demon invasion twice now. That was what the Deepdene Witch's powers were for – demon fighting. But they wouldn't work on an illness. At least, she was almost positive they wouldn't. She still hadn't figured out everything she could do with them.

Another thought she didn't really want to have slithered and wriggled its way into her brain. What if the flu epidemic – a few people had even called it a plague, whispering the word – what if it was actually a demon invasion? During the first invasion, several demon victims had been admitted to a mental hospital. If a demon presence in town could cause mental illness, was it possible a different demon could cause physical illness?

But every day there was a new doctor on the news, and most of them believed that the epidemic was a mutant strain of the flu. A couple of politicos were going with terrorism, but the majority of experts were behind the flu theory. *A demon isn't behind everything bad that happens in Deepdene*, Eve reminded herself.

Jess pulled her sunglasses back on. The frames were movie-star-in-hiding huge, hiding not just Jess's bright blue eyes, but her perfectly groomed eyebrows as well. She adjusted her lounger so that it lay flat, then stretched out on her stomach, her head angled towards Eve. 'I can wear a sundress for my date with Seth tonight, right?' she asked. She paused and smiled. 'My date. With Seth. Did you ever believe I'd be saying those words?'

Seth was a senior, and it seemed like he saw Jess as a kindergartener instead of a freshman, at least until a few months ago. Then, lightbulb moment – or maybe it should be called hormone moment – he realized she was all grown up.

'For probably the infinity-plus-one time, yes, I can believe you and Seth are going out,' Eve said, happy to have a more cheerful topic of conversation. 'I think pretty much everyone at Deepdene High has you two down as the new hot couple.'

Jess's smile widened into a grin. 'So, sundress? I know it's March, but with this weather . . .'

'You'd be crazy to wear anything else,' Eve replied. 'The white one with the little blue flowers. With your tan? Perfection.' She kissed her fingertips, getting a little taste of her coconut-scented sunscreen.

'Unless I get the . . . you know . . . between now and then,' Jess said. 'If I have to cancel and Seth breaks up with me, I'm going to kill Mr Dokey. Why did his life-long dream have to be going to Egypt, land of unexplained diseases? Why couldn't he have wanted to go to Paris, like a normal person?'

Eve laughed. 'Like us, you mean,' she said. Jess's parents had taken them to Paris two years ago and neither of them could wait to go back. 'I actually have trouble picturing Mr Dokey there.'

'True. He's not nearly *chic* enough,' Jess joked. 'But still. He could have gone to England at least. He wouldn't have brought anything nasty home from there.'

'Hmm, no. England isn't exotic enough for a geography teacher,' Eve commented. Most of the experts who'd weighed in thought that Mr Dokey had probably become infected with a rare disease while he was on vacation in Egypt. In February, he'd gotten permission to take a week off to go visit an archaeological dig, as long as he did a presentation about it for the school. A week or so after he returned, he'd become the first victim of the pla— of Flu X.

'What shoes are you going to wear?' Eve asked, getting back to the more pleasant subject of Jess's date attire. 'The strappy ones with—' The sound of the French doors opening interrupted her. She looked over and saw her mom stepping out onto the paving stones that snaked through the grass over to the pool area. She was carrying two smallish cardboard boxes.

'Hi, Mrs Evergold,' Jess called.

'Are you girls doing all right?' Eve's mother walked over and sat down on the edge of Eve's lounger, putting her hand against her daughter's forehead. 'You feel hot,' she announced.

'Um, there's a freak heatwave going on,' Eve reminded her, making her voice light and teasing, not wanting her mother to get even more worried about the flu than she already was. 'Everyone feels hot.'

Her mother laughed, but it came out sounding a little strained. 'It *is* hot. I should have factored that in,' she admitted. 'But I want you to take your temperature later. You should do it at least once a day. You too, Jess.'

Eve nodded. She couldn't help wondering what her mother would do if she did get a fever. It would probably mean that Eve had gotten Flu X. But then what? There was no cure, nothing that made it better, that anyone knew about. And that was terrifying. But at least no one had died from the disease yet.

'One of my colleagues told me that the doctors analysing the blood of the infected people have become ill themselves,' Eve's mother said. 'This disease is virulent. The speed at which it spreads . . . it's, well, it's frightening.'

Eve tried to remember the last time her mother had called anything frightening. Her dad was creeped out by any movie that had a shark – or mutant crocodile or anything else aquatic and deadly – in it. Plus, he was afraid of hairy spiders, and he totally admitted it. But nothing ever seemed to get to her mother.

'I also heard on the radio on my way home that the mayor is considering closing all the schools in town. I hope he does,' Mrs Evergold continued. 'With something so infectious, it's reckless to allow large groups of people to congregate.'

'School might close? For how long?' Jess exclaimed.

'I don't know. The town doesn't have any protocol in place for a situation like this.' Eve's mother stood up. 'But I want you both to start taking more pre-cautions.' She handed Eve and Jess the small boxes.

Eve opened hers and pulled out a disposable mask that hooked over the ears and covered the nose and mouth, like a surgeon's mask. 'Wear these whenever you're out of the house – school, Ola's, wherever. I'm going to go see if there's anything more on the news,' Eve's mother said, then returned inside.

'School had better close,' Jess muttered. 'Because I would not want to go walking in there wearing one of these.' She reached over and flicked the mask Eve had taken out of the box.

'You'll wear it when you're out though, right?' Eve asked. 'I don't want you getting sick.'

'Everywhere but on my date with Seth,' Jess promised. 'It would be impossible to kiss. And it doesn't match the clutch I'm planning to carry.' She set the box of masks down beside her. 'Let's just try to enjoy this amazing sun. There's no demon crisis, at least, so there's no reason we can't just stay here by the pool for now. *Without* our masks.'

Eve didn't mention that she'd considered the possibility that the plague *was* a demon crisis. All those doctors had to be right.

And if they turned out to be wrong, which Eve was sure they weren't, Jess would be there for her. Jess didn't have any supernatural demon-fighting powers, but that hadn't stopped her from being right at Eve's side the other two times demons had shown up in Deepdene. She'd been with Eve the day they learned that there was a portal between hell and earth right in their town. And she'd been there when Eve had managed to use her power to weave something like a psychic force field over the portal to keep all the nasties in hell where they belonged. If there was demon trouble, Jess always made it clear that it was her problem just as much as it was Eve's. One of the dozens of reasons Eve loved her friend.

'I'm going to check the school website. Maybe it'll say something about it closing.' Eve reached under the lounger where she'd stashed her pink Macbook Pro and pulled it out. A few clicks later and she was on the Deepdene High home page.

'Anything?' Jess asked.

'Just the usual. Lunch menu. Sports schedule,' Eve answered. 'Jenna's online. I'm going to IM her and see what she's heard.'

Jess grabbed her cell. 'I'll text Megan. Megan always knows everything.'

Eve's fingers danced over the keyboard as she wrote the IM to Jenna. *School might close. Heard?!?*

A response from Jenna popped up almost immediately. *Srsly???? So don't want to do bio hmwrk.*

*Gonna try 2 find confirmation. Get back 2 U*, Eve answered.

'Megan says she's watching the news with her mom. We're up to eighty-one sick people,' Jess told her, with the phone still to her ear. 'She says she hasn't heard anything about school closing. But in other gossip news, a while ago Briony's dad called her, looking for Briony. She didn't come home last night.'

'He must be freaking,' Eve said.

Jess held up one finger, listening to Megan, then she said goodbye and hung up. 'Megan said Briony's dad is really worried, but he thinks she probably took off to see the old boyfriend in Massachusetts. She's been on the phone with him a lot lately.'

'Yeah, she was talking about him the other day, and how her dad didn't approve.' Eve held her hands out, pretending they were weighing scales. 'So we have cute old boyfriend on one side, and a town with a plague and a disapproving dad on the other. I'm thinking—' She dropped the hand that represented Deepdene to the ground.

'Briony has to think this town is cursed,' Jess commented. 'She got here right when the hell hounds were on the loose. So first those murders and now Flu X. Even without the cute guy, I can understand why she'd bolt.'

'Hey, Luke's online.' Eve smiled as she saw his screen name pop up – Sinbad. He'd chosen it because he was a minister's son and so he knew sin was bad. And also Sinbad, the ancient heroic sailor, was kick-ass.

According to Luke, he'd battled, among other things, a Cyclops with teeth like a boar's tusks, and a snake so big it could swallow an elephant.

And Luke had battled demons side by side with Eve too. Like Jess, he had no powers. But, also like Jess, he didn't let that stop him. If there was badness to fight, he was there. Eve felt like she knew him so well, even though she had only met Luke at the beginning of school this year. He and his dad had moved to Deepdene from California so his father could take over as minister at Deepdene Church after the previous minister had died from cancer.

'Are you telling him you luuuuurve him?' Jess teased as Eve began writing an IM to Luke.

'Telling him about Briony, since they went out a couple of times,' Eve replied. Although she had to admit, at least to herself, that she had wondered once or twice if she was falling for Luke. She hoped not. The boy was a player – Briony was just one of the many girls he'd gone out with since he came to town – and getting involved with him as more than a friend would probably leave Eve with a broken heart.

The thing was, Luke was more than just a player. He was brave. He was smart. He was pretty sweet a lot of the time. And, yes, he was a complete cutie with his longish blond hair and his green eyes. Make that green eyes with little golden flecks. He was—

He was not answering her. How long did it take to answer an IM? Jenna had replied in about a second and a half. Eve could see he was online. To ignore her was just rude.

'Is Luke saying something bad? Is someone else sick?' Jess asked.

'No. He didn't answer yet,' Eve said. Because he was busy chatting with some other girl? He *was* a player. She couldn't let herself forget that.

'Oh. It's just that you just looked upset,' Jess commented, propping herself up on one elbow.

'There's a lot of upsetting stuff happening,' Eve reminded her. 'Eighty-one people sick. No known cure.' And Luke possibly blowing her off for some fun girl who'd never drag him into a demon beat-down.

Eve reached the end of her *Vogue*, and realized she didn't remember one thing that was in it. Not one pair of shoes. Not one bag. Usually as soon as she started flipping through a new issue, a shopping list began forming in her head. This time her head had been too full of the epidemic. *And Luke*, she admitted to herself. She let out a sigh.

'Want to do this relationship quiz?' Jess asked.

'Unlike you, I'm not in a relationship,' Eve pointed out.

'Just use Luke. It will help you decide if you should take him on as a boyfriend,' Jess answered.

Eve laughed. 'You sound like it's all my decision.'

'It is. I keep telling you that.' Jess pulled a pen out of her bag. 'I've seen the way he looks at you. You give the guy one encouraging word and he's yours. Guaranteed.' She looked down at her magazine. 'OK, first question. If your guy were a popsicle, what flavour would he be? A – Lime, B – Cherry, C – Orange, or D – Grape.'

'That's key in deciding if he's good relationship material?' Eve asked doubtfully.

'Absolutely. And Seth is definitely orange, like sunshine. Sunshine you want to lick,' Jess added. 'What about Luke?'

Eve wrinkled her nose. 'It's kind of a dumb question. I mean, no offence. But guys as popsicle flavours?'

'Just pick one.' Jess tapped her pen against her magazine.

'Lime, I guess.'

'Which happens to be your fave,' Jess commented. 'Your psychology is showing.'

'That isn't—'

The sound of Eve's cell ringing interrupted her, and she jumped to get it. Distraction was good. She didn't need to do any more thinking about Luke. Who couldn't even be bothered to answer a simple IM.

She glanced at the caller ID. Luke. Well, he hadn't answered her before, but calling her was even better, right? She couldn't help smiling. 'Hi, Luke,' she said as she picked up.

Jess smirked at her, a see-I-know-all smirk. Eve ignored it.

'What's up?' she asked Luke.

'Sorry I didn't answer you before,' Luke said. 'My dad . . . We just got back from the walk-in clinic. He has it. He almost passed out during the Wednesday men's lunch group.'

He was trying to hold it together, but Eve could hear the tremor in his voice. Of course he was freaking. It was his *dad*. And Luke had already lost his mother. He never talked about it. All Eve knew was that she'd died in a car accident when he was really young, about five years old.

'Oh no, Luke. That's horrible,' Eve exclaimed. 'His

dad. The flu,' she mouthed to Jess, and her friend's eyes darkened with concern.

'It pretty much had to happen,' Luke said quietly. 'I mean, he's the minister. It's his job to be around people. He spent the whole day yesterday making calls on everyone in the congregation who's down with it. This morning before the lunch too.'

'He's a good man, doing that,' Eve said. 'How bad is it?' *Stupid question,* she thought, nibbling at her lip the way she always did when she was nervous. If you had Flu X it was bad. Period.

'He's not feeling all that sick, but his fever's pretty high,' Luke told her. 'But, you know—'

'Yeah,' Eve answered. It didn't feel like there was anything else to say. 'I'm so sorry,' she added anyway. Why was it so hard to find the right words sometimes?

'Look, I know this is a big favour, but I was wondering . . .' Luke hesitated.

'I owe you a couple of dozen favours at least. What?' Eve prompted him.

'I need a place to stay. The doctor checked me over, and I'm fine. At least so far. But he wants me out of the house or else I'll definitely catch it too. The Deepdene town council has arranged for nursing

23

teams to give in-home care to all the infected people. They don't want sick and healthy people living in the same houses. So . . .'

Luke. In her house? For days? Eve couldn't tell if her fluttering heart meant she was thrilled or anxious beyond belief. 'That makes perfect sense,' she told him. 'Let me ask my mom. I'm sure she'll say you can stay.'

Jess sat up fast and grabbed Eve's arm. They had one of their eye conversations. Jess's eyes: *Luke is staying with you*? Eve's eyes: *OMG*. Just *OMG*.

'I thought I'd be able to stay with Ben Flood or one of the guys on the team.' Luke had joined the football team when he first moved to town, and then he moved on to basketball with everyone else when the season changed. 'But Ben's sick and so are a bunch of the other guys. We've had b-ball practice every day lately, and everyone's in the locker room together afterwards . . .'

'That's like a huge petri dish for germs,' Eve said, automatically repeating what her surgeon mother always said as her mind whirled with the pros and cons of a Luke stay-over.

'Yeah. It's no surprise the flu spread through most of the team,' Luke agreed. 'But I've been checked out by the doctor and am showing no signs – at least for now . . . Anyway, I didn't know who else to call.'

'I'm the first one you should have called. Have you ever been in Ben's room? The flu probably isn't the worst thing you could catch in there,' Eve told him. 'I'll check with my mom and call you back.'

'You've been in Ben's bedroom?' The volume on Luke's voice had gone up a few notches. *Is he jealous?* Eve wondered, and the thought made her smile.

'We were partners on an English project last year,' Eve said. 'I'm hanging up. Call you in a few.'

'Luke wants to stay here. With you?' Jess burst out the second Eve hung up.

'Yeah. The public health people don't want healthy people and people with the flu in the same house,' Eve answered.

'His dad. That part flew out of my head for a second. Poor Luke. I can't even imagine. I don't want to even imagine . . .' Jess shook her head.

'I know. I couldn't even come up with something decent to say to him. What are you supposed to say to someone whose father is that sick?' Eve asked.

'It's more about being there than about what you say, I think,' Jess answered. 'It'll be good for him to stay with you. Are you freaking about it though?'

25

'A little,' Eve admitted. 'Of course I want him to come if he needs a place to stay. It's just weird having a guy in your house.'

'A guy you like,' Jess corrected.

Eve didn't confirm or deny. And she still hadn't quite figured out if she was excited or anxious. 'I'm going to go ask my mom if it's OK.'

She crossed the patio, opened the sliding glass door, and headed into the living room. Her mother was watching CNN with the air conditioner cranked.

'Mom, Luke just called. His dad is sick – Flu X – and so Luke needs a place to stay. Would it be OK . . . ?'

She didn't have to say anything else. 'He's welcome as long as he needs to be here,' her mother told her. 'No one healthy should be in the same house as someone who's sick.' Mrs Evergold stood up and turned off the TV. 'I'll go get the guest room ready.'

Eve returned to the back yard and her lounger.

'She said yes, of course,' Jess said.

'Of course,' Eve answered. She'd never doubted that would be her mother's response. She picked up her iPhone and hesitated.

'It's going to be all good. You look adorable when you brush your teeth.' Jess gave Eve's shoulder a pat.

'I'm not letting him see me brush my teeth,' Eve shot back.

Jess held up her hands. 'OK, OK, I just thought it would be cute, like in *Bring It On*, when Kirsten and Jesse were brushing their teeth together and taking turns spitting.' Jess had seen every cheerleader film ever made. She considered it her cheerleader duty. Which meant Eve had seen all of them too.

'Good scene. Still not letting him see me spit,' Eve answered. She took a deep breath and called Luke. He answered on the first ring. 'OK, get your stuff and come here,' Eve told him. 'Mom says you can stay as long as you need to.'

'Great. That's great. Thanks. I'll be over in a couple of hours,' he replied. 'I want to make sure my dad's nursing team gets here and all. You know, it's good that I'm staying with you instead of one of the guys. It'll make it easier to talk about *stuff*.'

Eve instantly knew what he meant. She was getting almost as telefriendic – a word she and Jess had come up with for friends being able to read each other's minds – with Luke as she was with Jess. 'You're thinking that the plague is demon related,' she said.

An expression of alarm flashed over Jess's face. 'It's the flu!' she cried.

'Wait, I'm putting you on speaker. Jess has to hear or she'll implode.' Eve turned to Jess. 'If you see my mom coming out here, tell me.'

'You think we're in the middle of a demon plague?' Jess exclaimed. 'Luke, the doctors are all saying it's a mutant strain of the flu. They're working on a vaccine. It's bad, but it's not demon bad.'

'Tell that to my dad,' Luke snapped. 'Sorry,' he said immediately. 'I'm just—'

'Worried about him,' Jess supplied, her voice tender.

'Yeah,' Luke answered. 'And maybe I'm just wanting it to be a demon thing because it would give me – us – something to fight. I hate not being able to do anything for my father.'

'We get that,' Eve told him. 'It definitely went through my mind that the plague might be connected to a demon.'

'It did?' Jess exclaimed, outraged. 'And you didn't tell me?'

'We were both already scared,' Eve said. 'And pretty much right away I decided all those doctors couldn't be wrong about the epidemic being a weird strain of the flu.'

'So why did you think demons at all?' Jess asked.

'Because it's Deepdene, home to a portal to hell,' Eve said. 'And the last two times really bad stuff happened it was because a demon came through the portal. Plus I was thinking how the first demons caused mental illness and that maybe a demon causing physical illness was a possibility.'

'Exactly,' Luke jumped in. 'And then there's the bizarre weather. It's the hottest temperature on record for March in the Hamptons, by almost fifteen degrees. It's nearly a hundred today. The record for the beginning of March is eighty-three.'

Jess pressed one hand over her face. 'Demons,' she whispered.

'Maybe not,' Eve said. 'I think the first thing we have to do is check the portal to make sure it's still blocked.' The wargs – demon-faced hellhounds – hadn't come back through the electric spider web that she'd woven over the opening, so she'd assumed it was holding.

'Good idea,' Luke told her. Jess nodded in agreement. 'But even if your net is still in place, it doesn't mean a demon couldn't come through. Maybe it's only strong enough to keep out lesser demons, like the wargs. Maybe a more powerful demon could stroll right through, no problem.'

'You are definitely not an orange popsicle,' Eve muttered.

'What?' Luke asked.

'Nothing,' Eve said. But he so was not a beam of lickable sunshine right now. He was more like a dark cloud. She got it though. She could see why he'd want something to fight to save his dad. 'Let me check the portal first. Jess and I will go over right now. When you get here, we can decide what to do next.'

'Sounds good. Thanks. See you guys soon,' Luke replied.

'See you.' Eve snapped her phone closed and stood up. 'Feel like taking a walk to the edge of hell?' she asked Jess.

'Absolutely,' her friend answered, tying a sarong around her hips and pulling on the oversized white shirt she liked to use as a cover-up. Eve slipped into the T-shirt and denim shorts she'd had on when they first came out to the back yard.

'And then we have to go shopping,' Eve announced.

'For new pyjamas, right?' Jess knew her way too well.

'I've been needing some,' Eve said.

'Right. It has nothing to do with the fact that Luke's going to be sleeping over,' Jess teased her.

'Of course not!' But Eve didn't even manage to convince herself, never mind Jess. Luke was sleeping over. Which meant that they might run into each other in the hallway or the bathroom or on a midnight-snack fridge raid. Demon investigation might be advisable. But pyjama prep was *mandatory*.

# Chapter Two

A shudder rippled through Eve, and she shivered as she and Jess stepped onto the wildly overgrown lawn in front of the Medway mansion. Make that the *remains* of the Medway mansion – the place was nothing more than piles of brick and masonry scattered about like a giant had stomped on them. One of the worst nights of her life had happened in that house, back when it was still standing, and just to put the cherry on top of the horribleness, it was a night that had started out feeling like one of the best.

Mal – gorgeous, sexy Mal – had invited Eve over for dinner, a dinner he was cooking just for her. It had been so insanely romantic. Until she realized that Mal was in fact Malphas, a Prince of Hell, and she'd had to use her power to blast him into a few wisps of smoke.

'Thinking about Mal?' Jess asked, being tele-friendic, as usual.

'Malphas,' Eve corrected her. She preferred to use his true name, his demon name. Not the name they had all known him by at school. 'And, yeah, I was. I still can't believe I dated a demon.'

'Why not? He was unbelievably cute. Pretty much every girl in school wanted to go out with him,' Jess reminded her. 'It's not like he walked around smelling like brimstone – whatever brimstone smells like – with horns sprouting out of his head. You didn't know he was a demon.'

'Actually, he did always smell. Like wood-smoke,' Eve said. 'Not brimstone. Or maybe that's how brimstone smells?' She frowned. 'I smelled wood-smoke when the wargs were out too.' She gave a long sniff. 'But right now, nothing.'

'Another reason to think the plague is a virus or something,' Jess said.

'Come on. Let's do this, then it's shopping time.' Eve wanted to shop, but even more, she wanted to get away from ruins of the Medway manor and the portal. She grabbed Jess's hand and pulled her towards a gothic stone arch. The portal, the only part of the mansion that hadn't crumbled when Eve had finished Malphas.

They stopped a few metres away. 'Anything could

be over there,' Jess whispered.

She was right. Who knew what was on the other side, invisible to their eyes. Any one of the creatures from hell could be crouched there, waiting for a chance to come through.

Eve nervously flexed her fingers, ready to blast her power if she needed to. Jess noticed and asked, 'Are you sensing something?'

'Nuh-uh,' Eve reassured her. She needed to get closer to the portal to check that her web of power was still in place. Until she touched it, it would remain hidden.

Luke had cleared most of the rubble in front of the arch when they'd first discovered it, so it was easy to walk up to the portal. When she was a breath away from it, she tried to ignore the words carved into the stone – words that she could read easily even though Luke and Jess said they looked like hieroglyphics to them.

Apparently one of the bonuses of being the Deepdene Witch was that Eve could understand Demonese. The words were basically just instructions to the Medway family about how they had to open the portal every hundred years. Helena, a girl in their year at school, had been the most recent descendant of Lord Medway. She'd opened the portal and let the hellhounds into Deepdene, thinking she could control them. Instead, they'd destroyed her, ripping her to shreds.

Looking at the words reminded Eve of how different she was now that she had grown into the witchiness she'd inherited from her great-great-multiple-great-grandmother. *OK, Ms Superwitch, get to it*, she thought.

Eve reached out and tried to put her hand through the arch. Things on the other side looked normal, just like she was staring through an open doorway. But as soon as her fingers touched the air within the archway, a spark flew out, sending faint, fuzzy golden lines crisscrossing all across the opening with a series of crackling sounds.

She looked over her shoulder at Jess. 'Does it seem—'

'Different,' Jess said. 'Yeah. In a weaker kind of way. The lines are fuzzy and they weren't before.'

'They're more translucent too,' Eve added. 'But it's still working. I can't put my hand through, so the other side should be blocked too.' She frowned. 'I don't like that it's fading, though. I want to try to juice it up some more.'

Eve closed her eyes, trying to remember what it felt like when she'd created the web the first time. Her power had felt softer somehow, warm rather than hot. When she attacked demons it felt scalding, although the heat didn't bring her any pain.

She focused on gathering her power together. Her hair began to gently undulate around her face, as if she was underwater. Her skin started to tingle, her tongue and the backs of her eyes too. *It's time*, she thought, and released the power.

Rays of golden light began to flow from the tips of her fingers. Eve pressed her hands against the portal arch, feeling the carved markings against her palms. The stone was cold, even though the day was sweltering, but it began to warm as Eve's power entered it.

'It's working,' Jess said softly as the golden strands of the web grew brighter and crisper.

Eve didn't let go of the arch. As she continued to fill it with her power, more rays of light were added to the web, weaving over and under the ones that had already been there, until the portal opening looked like it was completely covered by a dense golden tapestry.

With a sigh of satisfaction, she pulled her hands away. The golden light slowly faded, but Eve knew that the opening to the portal was still completely covered.

'Can I just say that you have moments of total awesomeness?' Jess asked.

Eve smiled as she turned towards her friend. 'You too.'

'Well, yeah,' Jess agreed with a wink. 'Now on to the stores!'

Before Eve could take a step, she heard a dull *thunk*. She jerked her head towards the sound, and saw a chunk of stone from the ruin of the dovecote roll into the high weeds. 'That scared me to—'

Another sound interrupted her, a softer sound, but one that also came from the crumbled stone remains of the nearby dovecote. Jess gave a yelp of surprise when a man stumbled into sight. He wore several layers of clothes, despite the heat, all stained and dirty.

'What are you doing here?' Eve blurted, although she and Jess had no right to be on the Medway property either.

The man didn't answer. Jess and Eve moved closer together. He lurched towards them, then veered away, heading for the front gate, muttering as he went. His words were so slurred and raspy Eve couldn't understand them.

'Do you think that guy is living here?' Jess asked when he'd disappeared from sight. 'I mean, do you think he's homeless?'

'Maybe,' Eve said. 'He was really skinny under all those clothes, and it didn't seem like he's had access to a shower in a good while. What I want to know is – did he see anything?' She wiggled her fingers in front of Jess's face to indicate her power.

'He didn't act like he had,' Jess said. 'He wasn't really staring over here or anything.'

'But if he was back there behind all those stones from the dovecote, he might have,' Eve answered.

'Did you get a sniff of him when he headed by?' Jess said. 'Eau de Beer mixed with garbage. I hope he hasn't had to go dumpster-diving to eat. That would be so sad.'

'He did smell like he'd been drinking,' Eve agreed. 'Not good, but a lot better than Eau de Wood-smoke.'

'So much better. And if he did happen to see something – well, he probably walks around seeing groovy glowing lights all the time,' Jess said. Eve pulled out her cell. 'Giving Luke an update?' Jess asked.

'I'll text him in a sec,' Eve said. 'Right now I'm setting a reminder alarm. I'm going to be checking the portal once a week to make sure the block is still strong.'

Jess laughed.

'What?' Eve asked.

'It just seems weird to do witch stuff on your phone,' her friend said. 'Although probably if Lord Medway was trying to make a deal with Malphas today, he'd use a cell too.'

'I'm thinking demons don't have access to phones on the other side.' Eve turned back and ran her fingers over the web again, just to see it spark, just to prove it was still there. Lord Medway must have been truly and deeply crazy to have made a deal with Malphas – or with any demon. Demons were bad news. But then to create a portal to hell and swear that your children and grandchildren would open it every hundred years to let Malphas return? It was like putting a curse on your own family! Lord Medway should have known better. Anyone should have known better. And Lord Medway was a pilgrim. They were supposed to be all religious, right? Not that you had to be religious to know that opening a door to hell was bad.

'OK, now on to important business,' Jess said, pulling Eve away from the portal – and her dark thoughts. 'Shopping!'

They started down Medway Lane, which led in a big loop from the downtown area of Main Street to the beachfront properties and back again. It wasn't a terribly long walk, but in this heat, Eve felt like they couldn't get to the stores – and the air conditioning – fast enough.

'Ice cream first or shopping first?' Jess asked.

'Shopping,' Eve said. 'The ice cream would just melt, anyway.'

'OK, so . . . PJs. Were you thinking actual pyjama pyjamas or are you open to nightgowns?' Jess asked.

'Pyjama pyjamas,' Eve answered as they walked, trying to stay in the shade of the maple trees that lined the road. 'Nightgowns seem . . .' She shrugged.

'Like you're trying too hard,' Jess agreed. 'You want to look your cutest without seeming like you're trying to look cute at all. Easy-peasy. Luke would think you looked cute if you came to breakfast in those Care Bear PJs you like to wear when you're sick.'

'Luke is never seeing those,' Eve said. She narrowed her eyes at Jess. 'Luke is never *hearing* about them, either. Or there will be consequences. Consequences involving Seth finding out about that stalkerette notebook you kept on him for an entire year back in seventh grade.'

Jess held her hands up in surrender, laughing. 'The Care Bears are in the vault with all the other best friend secrets,' she promised.

They reached the corner of Medway and Main, which was the beginning of Deepdene's tiny shopping area. Pretty much every store and restaurant in town was located on these few Main Street blocks.

Eve stopped and took one of the masks her mother had given her out of her purse. 'If my mom catches me around a bunch of people without this, I'm doomed.'

Jess hesitated. 'Come on. Do it, Jess,' Eve urged. 'I think this is one of those very rare times where we're both going to have to put safety above fashion. I don't want you getting sick on me.'

'It's just that there aren't a bunch of people,' Jess answered.

'On Main Street?' Eve exclaimed. But Jess was right. There were only two people in sight – a woman carrying a truly amazing number of bags out of the wine and cheese shop, a long scarf wrapped over her mouth, and Mr Enslow, who stood in front of his hardware store, arms crossed over his chest.

It was just . . . wrong. On a Wednesday afternoon, half the people from school should be over here at

Ola's or Java Nation, and there were always people shopping the boutiques, even in the off-season.

'Creepy,' Eve said.

'Do you think she left anything in the cheese place?' Jess asked, watching the woman as she struggled to her car with her many, many bags.

'I went to the grocery store with my mom yesterday, and there were lots of gaps on the shelves. My mom said people go into a hoarding mentality when there's a crisis,' Eve replied.

'I guess it's good our pantry is full,' Jess said. 'Although with Peter in the house ... You know how he eats.'

Peter was Jess's younger-by-one-year brother. And Eve had seen him eat many times – almost always with his mouth open to gross her out. He could definitely put the groceries away.

'So, back to the vital business of pyjamas,' Jess said. 'How about we start at the Ralph Lauren boutique?'

'Sounds like a plan.' Eve dangled the elastic of her mask over one finger as they walked over to the boutique. If she got into a crowded spot, she'd put it on. But it really didn't look like that was going to happen.

She took a deep, appreciative breath as they stepped

into the shop. Some people raved about new-car smell, but for Eve, nothing beat the new-clothes smell. It should be made into a perfume. She'd buy it for sure.

Jess flipped through a rack of pyjama sets. 'I love the pyjamas here. They're so retro, like guys wear in old, old movies, except they're tailored for a girl body.' Jess's voice sounded really loud in the almost deserted store. It was just her and Eve and one sales clerk. She held up a pair with simple blue stripes for Eve to look at. 'Definitely cute. Definitely not trying too hard. Definitely sexy.'

'Sexy isn't on the list of requirements,' Eve told her. 'Luke isn't my boyfriend, remember?'

'I remember that he's your lime popsicle,' Jess replied. 'And I also remember lime popsicles are your favourite.'

*Footsteps.*

Luke turned round, automatically on guard. He couldn't shake the feeling a demon was behind the plague, and right now every sound he heard seemed like a potential threat. But it was just Eve and Jess, walking up the sidewalk of Sycamore Street towards the Evergold house, loaded down with colourful shopping bags. 'Is there anything left for sale on Main Street?' Luke called, smiling at them.

Eve raised one eyebrow as she grinned back. 'You're not exactly travelling light, either,' she commented as she and Jess reached him.

Luke hitched his backpack higher on his shoulder. It kept sliding off, and the straps of his gym bag had just about worn a groove in the palm of his left hand. 'I brought half the stuff in my wardrobe,' he admitted. 'I don't know how long I'll have to stay. And I'm not allowed back at the rectory, the sheriff said. They have the whole place, and the church, blocked off with police tape. No one gets through until there's some kind of inoculation against Flu X. Or a cure.'

'Which they *will* find. Soon. I know it,' Eve told him. Jess nodded her agreement.

They were sweet. Big, fat liars, but sweet.

'It just feels wrong to be over here,' Luke said. 'I should be with my dad. I mean, I'm really grateful to you, Eve. But it's strange, being kicked out of my own house.'

'At least you know your father is being taken care of,' Jess said. 'He probably feels better knowing he can't infect you.'

'Plus, my mom completely agrees that you

shouldn't be near your dad. She's happy that you're staying with us,' Eve reassured him. 'I know my dad will be too. Don't worry about it at all. This is your home as long as you need to stay.'

'Thanks,' Luke answered. He was glad Eve had said he could stay, but now that he was standing in front of her he suddenly wondered if it would be weird. Half the time – at least – that he was around her he had this impulse to kiss her. If he were around her *all* the time . . . *Not your biggest problem right now*, he told himself. 'And you're right, Jess,' he added. 'My father wanted me out of there even more than the CDC people.' The Center for Disease Control had recently sent in a team to help control the outbreak.

'It's not going to help him if you get sick as well,' Eve gently reminded him.

'I know. But still.' Luke let out a sigh that felt like it had started in the soles of his feet. *Get a grip*, he ordered himself. 'Anyway, at least I can do something here. I finished entering all the demon info we've gathered over the past few months onto my laptop, and I brought the books and journals we found hidden in the church. I'm not done translating everything, but I'm getting there. We'll figure out how to stop this.'

Eve's forehead wrinkled in confusion. 'Didn't you get my text? We checked the portal, and the force field thingy, or the fence, or whatever we're calling it, was still live. I gave it some extra juice to make sure it stays that way. Plus I haven't smelled any wood-smoke.'

'Yeah, but even if the portal is closed, demons could've gotten in another way,' Luke pointed out. 'Helena wrote in her diary that she'd been able to summon demons, remember? That proves the portal isn't the only way it can happen.'

'True. It seems like every few weeks we're running into new things we thought could never happen,' Eve answered. 'I'm still feeling like the most logical scenario is Mr Dokey bringing Flu X back from Egypt, but we should stay on guard. Maybe investigate a little.'

'Helena's dead,' Jess reminded them. 'And she was the last of the Medway descendants. Do you think there's another wacko family in town who thinks it's a good idea to try and make friends with demons?'

'No . . .' Luke wasn't entirely sure what he thought, other than that the intense heat and the contagious disease outbreak were *not* natural. Somehow, a demon was behind what was happening in town. Luke could feel it in his gut, like a jagged stone.

'Let's get this stuff inside,' Eve suggested, starting for her front door. Luke knew she didn't fully agree with him, but at least she was open to the possibility that there was another demon they might have to fight.

'Helena's story is just one example,' Luke said. 'I bet the Order knows hundreds of ways that demons can get from hell to our world.' He jerked his backpack into place again. 'Maybe we should email them an update on what's going on.'

The Order was an ancient association of those dedicated to hunting and killing demons. Luke, Jess, and Eve had learned of its existence when the wargs had invaded. The Order had sent Willem Payne, one of its members, to investigate the death of Kyle Rakoff, who was on the Deepdene High football team with Luke. It turned out that Kyle had been killed by a pack of the hell hounds, and Willem too had been slain by the creatures. Moments before he died, he'd given Luke his sword, a weapon that could kill demons.

'I'm not sure we're at the point where we should get the Order involved,' Eve answered. She let her hand drop before it reached the doorknob and turned to face Luke. 'I think we should wait until we have some evidence that there's definitely something super-natural going on.'

'But they gave us their contact info for a reason,' Luke protested. 'For all we know, the Order has info about a demon that causes people to get sick. Maybe something like this has happened before in another town. Even if it hasn't, I bet they'll have some ideas on what we have to do to stop it.'

'We can talk about it more inside,' Eve said, opening the front door. 'Mom, Luke's here!' she called, her voice echoing through the big house. There was no answer.

Luke rested his heavy gym bag on the polished hardwood floor. Eve's place was about five times bigger than the little rectory where he lived with his dad. Maybe her mother couldn't hear her from the other side of the house.

'Mom?' she called again.

'Wait, didn't my mom rope your parents into the planning meeting tonight?' Jess asked. She glanced over at Luke. 'My mother runs practically every charity in Deepdene. She's good at guilting people into being helpful. And now that your dad is—'

She clapped her hand over her mouth, her blue eyes wide with embarrassment.

'Now that my dad is sick, she has to take over the patient outreach,' he finished for her. 'Visiting infected people and all that. It's OK. I know my father would appreciate it.'

'Well, this meeting is about more than just outreach,' Eve said. She picked up Luke's gym bag and headed for the curved staircase. 'I totally forgot, Jess, but you're right. My mom said she's going to organize all the doctors in town to take shifts at the clinic, whether they practise there or not. And my dad's going to the meeting straight from work. He's good with organizing. He's all about the flow charts and back-up plans.'

'Deepdene's going to need them with the way the infection is spreading. I saw a bunch of other houses cordoned off on my way over here,' Luke answered, following Eve. He grabbed the back of the heavy bag to help her lift it up the steps.

'We saw some too, when we were walking back from the Medway mansion,' Jess said. 'Do we know who else has gotten sick? Have you heard anything?'

'I got a text that the coach is down,' Luke said. 'There have to be other people the way this is spreading, but I haven't heard any more names.'

'It could be anyone – anyone from school, just

anyone.' He could hear the fear in Jess's voice. He wished he could come up with something to say to reassure her. But of course it could happen to anyone. It had just happened to his dad.

Upstairs, Eve opened the second door on the left. 'Guest room,' she told him. Luke carted his stuff inside with her help.

'I can't believe you carried all that over here by yourself,' Eve said.

'I thought about bringing the sword too,' Luke answered. 'But I've been keeping it hidden in the crypt under the church so my dad won't stumble across it. The public health people practically kicked me off the property, so I couldn't get it before I left.'

It was a special weapon, and with it feeling like darkness was converging on the town again, Luke wished now he had it close by. Payne had believed that only that sword – and twelve others just like it – had the strength to kill a demon, but he'd had to reconsider when he saw what Eve could do with her bare hands – her bare hands and her inherited power from the first Deepdene Witch.

'If it turns out we need the sword, we'll find a way to get it,' Eve told him. 'OK, so the chest of drawers is empty. The closet is mostly empty. You can put your stuff wherever you want to.'

Luke pulled open the closet door. 'Well, it will be a little tight, but it'll do,' he joked. 'That's the biggest closet I've ever seen!'

'All the times we've been in Evie's room and you haven't looked in her closet?' Jess exclaimed. 'It's a must-see. Come on.' She playfully dragged him down the hall to Eve's room and threw open the door to the walk-in closet.

Luke drew in a breath. 'You weren't kidding,' he exclaimed.

Every time he'd been in Eve's room the closet door had been closed, and he'd never given any thought to what was behind it. Closets were just closets . . . except for this one. It was ridiculously huge.

'Are you sure *this* isn't the guest room?' Luke joked. 'Or maybe the stockroom for all the stores on Main?'

'Girls need more stuff than boys,' Eve said.

'Clearly.' He liked to give Eve a hard time about the amount of money she spent on all that girl stuff, but, if he was completely honest with himself, he kinda liked how much she and Jess loved their fashion.

But this wasn't the time for fun. 'Can we go back to

talking about the Order?' he asked. 'I still think it's worth getting them involved.'

'How about if the three of us do some research first?' Eve suggested. 'If we find anything that points to a demon, we'll go to them. Not that we'll need them. If there is a demon in Deepdene again, we'll do what we did the last two times. We'll kick its ass back to hell.'

Luke felt a rush of gratitude. The rock in his gut seemed to get a little lighter.

'The three of us,' Jess agreed. She glanced at her watch. 'But I can't demon-research right this second. I have to get home. I'm supposed to meet Seth in an hour, and I can't go like this.' She gestured to the sarong she had wrapped around her hips.

'Seth would be one lucky guy if you did,' Luke said, ducking out of the way as Jess tried to swat him on the arm, laughing.

So he was going to be alone. All alone with Eve. Which would be fine, if he could only accept that she saw him as some kind of a gal pal.

He'd tried to accept it. He'd gone out with the new girl, Briony, a few times. And a couple of other girls. But it was always the same – the whole time he was with one of those other girls, there was a part of him that was doing a compare and contrast with Eve. And Eve came out ahead every single time.

Luke glanced over at Eve, and she was looking at him. She immediately turned away, reaching over to shut her closet door. Jess cleared her throat, but she didn't say anything, which was unusual for her. Luke knew the silence was getting awkward, and he wondered if Jess could tell that he was a little nervous about being left alone with Eve . . . in Eve's room.

Jess gave a little nod, as if she'd decided something. 'Why don't you guys come out with Seth and me?'

'No way. It's a date,' Eve protested. 'You two should be alone.'

'Yeah, Seth would not appreciate us crashing. And we have research,' Luke added. Plus, being out with Jess and Seth would feel like a double date. That would not help with his acceptance of being Eve's nothing-more-than-a-friend.

'You still have to eat, research or not.' Jess pointed at Eve, then at Luke. 'You're coming.'

Luke had never heard her sound so bossy. He was almost afraid to argue.

'I guess we're going,' Eve said, glancing at Luke. 'Which means I have to get ready too.' She turned to Jess. 'Striped jersey high-low hem?'

'Of course,' Jess answered. 'Maybe with the Miu Miu patent leather two-tone platforms?'

Eve nibbled her bottom lip, considering. Luke turned his eyes away. Did she have to do that? The move completely killed him. It always made him think about her lips and how much he'd like to kiss her. 'Maybe too matchy-matchy?'

Jess nodded. 'Probably. How about the rattan Pradas?'

'Not the espadrilles,' Eve said.

'Please. Do I look to you like I've lost my mind?' Jess cried. 'The red matte with the knot.'

'OK, I officially have no idea what you two are talking about,' Luke burst in. 'Did you slip into some kind of Eve–Jess code?'

The girls laughed. 'You could say that,' Jess replied. 'Come on, cutie-pie. Eve needs her privacy.' She took his arm and led him out of Eve's room, shutting the door behind them. 'See you at Nikolai's in an hour. At least it's still open! A couple of the Main Street places have decided to close for the duration.' She gave him a little wave as she started towards the stairs.

'Jess! Wait.' Luke shoved his hair off his forehead as she turned back to him. 'Do I need to . . . I've never been to that restaurant. It's kind of fancy, isn't it?

Should I change? That's what you two were talking about, right? Clothes?'

'Mostly it was about shoes,' Jess answered. She opened the door to the guest room. 'Come on, I'll make you pretty.'

'You better not,' Luke warned, with a grin.

Jess dumped the contents of Luke's backpack and gym bag onto the bed, and then stared down at the heap of clothes as if they were pieces to a giant puzzle.

'This,' she said about five seconds later, tossing a grey T-shirt at him. 'The jeans you have on, which do amazing things for your butt. And that jacket Eve bought you after she set your old one on fire with her woo-woo. Also . . .' Jess rummaged around in her purse and pulled out something that looked like a super-big tube of lipstick. She pulled off the top and, before Luke could protest, ran the tube over his hair.

'Hey!' Luke jerked his head back.

'You asked for my help,' Jess reminded him. She patted his cheek. 'Don't worry. It's just a little hair wax. I want your hair to be a little piecier.'

'I have no idea what that means,' Luke told her.

'Just trust me.' Jess held out her hands and raised her eyebrows.

Reluctantly, Luke lowered his head to give her

better access to the hair. She wiggled her fingers around on his head while he tried not to squirm. 'Done,' she said after a minute. 'And perfect. Once you change into your Jess Meredith-styled outfit, you'll look exactly like the kind of guy who should be taking Eve for at date at Nikolai's. And now I've got to go work my magic on myself. See you there!'

*A date.* Luke's stomach flipped at Jess's words. As soon as she was gone, he pulled off his shirt, careful not to screw up the work she had done on his hair. His stomach felt a little tight, and his mouth was the tiniest bit dry. Which was how his stomach and his mouth always reacted to a first date.

But this wasn't a date of any kind. This was eating dinner with Eve and some friends, and that was something he'd done a bunch of times before. And it hadn't required hair wax.

Luke's stomach and his mouth weren't convinced by that logic. They remained in first-date mode.

*How long before Eve's ready to go?* he wondered. What was the conversion rate between the time it took a guy to get ready and the time it took for a girl? Especially a girl who had a closet so big it might as well be an excavation site.

Luke grabbed his cell. It had only been about an

hour since he'd seen his dad, but he wanted to check in. He and his dad, they were a team. All they had was each other.

He hesitated. *Maybe calling is a bad idea*, Luke thought. He didn't want to wake his father up. He decided to text instead. OFF TO DINNER WITH E AND J, he typed. CALL ME IF YOU'RE BORED.

Boredom was the least of his father's worries, and Luke knew it. But it was their style to keep things light.

*We'll find the cause of the plague*, Luke promised himself. *And we'll end this thing before anyone gets sicker.*

# Chapter Three

'There they are,' Eve said, pointing across Nikolai's back patio. Jess and Seth had already been shown to a table for four, right under the huge weeping willow that grew in the centre of the dining area, its trunk rising through a hole in the wooden deck. Eve gave some of its feathery leaves a friendly brush as she and Luke walked towards their friends. The tree was probably even older than the building, and that had been built a hundred years ago. Eve imagined the willow's roots stretching out below all the tables, across the lawn, and underneath the brick paving stones of the walkway that led down to the creek.

Nikolai's was the most beautiful restaurant in Deepdene. Eve had never seen it with more than one or two empty tables until now. Tonight there was only one other occupied table on the large deck. At least it wasn't so crowded she felt obliged to wear her mask.

'Wow, it looks like Jess has been swallowing lit candles or something,' she said softly to Luke, slowing down to take in her best friend's face. 'She's so happy, she's glowing from the inside.' Actually Seth's eyes looked extra-bright too. So sweet.

Luke pulled out Eve's chair for her. The move surprised her a little. But why should it have? Luke was a player. With the number of dates he'd been on, of course he'd picked up a few good moves.

'I've never eaten here before,' Luke commented as he sat down next to her. 'It's, um, nice.' Eve noticed that his voice was higher than usual, as if he was a little nervous. Was he thinking about his dad? Worrying?

'It is. It's the best place in town,' Jess answered with a giant smile. Eve had to laugh. She suspected that Jess would think anyplace she and Seth were together was the best place.

'Hey, did you guys hear that Sydney Granger is sick now?' Seth asked. He looked over at Luke. 'Sorry about your dad, man.' He pulled at the neck of his T-shirt, as if it was feeling too tight.

'Thanks,' Luke answered.

'I just found out about Sydney. I got a text from Rose right before we left. She said Syd has a fever, so . . .' Eve let her words trail off. They all knew what a fever meant. That was one more kid from school down with Flu X.

'I want to propose a motion,' Jess said.

'A motion?' Seth asked.

'Yes. A formal motion,' Jess replied. 'I move that we don't talk about the – the you-know-what – just until we finish dinner. Can I get a second?'

Eve raised her hand. She figured Luke could use an hour or so without talking about the disease. He was probably thinking about it constantly.

Luke chuckled. 'Moved and seconded. Motion passes!'

'So what should we talk about instead? Or maybe we shouldn't even bother to talk.' Seth leaned in and gave Jess a kiss.

'I guess we should talk about food. I think our waiter is coming over,' Luke said. He picked up a menu. Eve checked out the table and realized she didn't have a menu. No problem; she leaned closer to Luke and read over his shoulder. Then she realized that to anybody glancing over at them, she and Luke probably looked as couple-y as Jess and Seth. She pulled away quickly.

'I don't know what to go for,' Seth said. 'I guess I'm

60

not that hungry. When it's really hot I never feel like eating.'

'I don't know why I'm bothering with the menu. I almost always get a salad and stuffed vine leaves,' Eve said.

'Creature of habit,' Luke teased.

'You probably order something different every time you eat out. I know you like variety,' she teased back.

'Luke has a reputation as a player,' Jess explained to Seth. Since he was a senior, he probably wasn't up on all the freshman gossip. 'Me, I just think he's just searching for the right girl.' She gave Eve a significant look that Eve hoped neither of the guys picked up on. They probably didn't. Guys were pretty unobservant a lot of the time.

'I'm happy to see you here. Welcome,' the waiter said as he stepped up to them. He wore a safety mask over his mouth, which was why it took Eve a moment to realize that their waiter was Nikolai, fourth generation from the Nikolai who had started the restaurant. 'I wasn't sure if anyone would come tonight,' he continued. 'But I find food comforting.' He patted his round belly. 'I thought others might too. I have masks for anyone who wants them. The cook is wearing one too.' He ran his finger across his mask. Someone – maybe Nikolai himself – had used a marker to draw some big purple grapes on it.

They gave Nikolai their order. 'I'm glad you stayed open,' Jess called after him as he headed back inside.

He waved without turning round. 'Enjoy the beautiful night,' he called back.

It really was beautiful – warm, but not brutally hot the way it had been earlier because in March the sun went down early. The sky was so clear that Eve felt like she could reach up and touch the stars. A faint breeze was coming up from the creek that led down to the beach, bringing that tangy ocean smell with it.

The breeze flipped a lock of Jess's blonde hair onto her cheek. Seth immediately reached over and tucked it behind her ear. Eve felt a wave of . . . not jealousy, but something more like longing. She didn't begrudge Jess what she had with Seth, not at all. Eve was happy for her bestie. She just wished she had a guy who would look at her the way Seth looked at her friend, eyes all starry.

No, that wasn't it. Or it wasn't completely it. Eve knew there were guys at school who liked her and who would give her the Seth-look if she gave them the opportunity. But she didn't want the look from any of those guys. She wanted the look from a guy she could give the look back to. She wanted to find a guy she could all-out love who would all-out love her back.

A few minutes later, Nikolai came back with their drinks. 'I'm doing a little of everything tonight. My staff are—' He shook his head. 'That's not talk for a meal, especially not for my love birds.' He walked back inside again.

Eve smiled, trying to hide her embarrassment. Obviously Nikolai thought she and Luke were a couple. And Jess was actively campaigning for Eve to get together with Luke. She insisted that they were in love – or at least luuuurve – with each other already. Which they totally weren't. Although Eve had to admit, she'd been showing some symptoms of love sickness. Like the urgent desire for new pyjamas as soon as she knew Luke would be a house guest. And the way she was hyper-aware of every girl he so much as spoke to at school. If she reached over and put her hand on his arm right now, how would he react? Would he be glad she'd given him a signal? Would they become the couple they appeared to be, just like that?

'You like the way I did Luke's hair, don't you, Evie?' Jess asked. 'You've been checking him out since we sat down.' *Very subtle, Jess*, Eve thought. She knew her friend was doing what she could to make the couple thing happen because she thought Eve and Luke would be great together.

She felt her face go warm. She'd been thinking about Luke, but she hadn't realized she'd been staring. 'Did you use wax or gel?' she asked, trying to play it off as if she'd been deep in thought about Luke's hair and not Luke himself.

'Now *I* want to make a motion,' Seth cut in. 'Can we not talk about hair products?' He took a long, long drink of the ginger beer he'd ordered.

Luke immediately raised his hand. 'Seconded!'

Jess pouted playfully. 'Fine. No-fun motion passes. We'll have to discuss something besides contagious diseases or beauty routines. What else is there?'

Eve was finding it hard to think of anything to say. Why was it that the more you liked a guy, the more difficult it became to decide what to say? Back when she first met Luke, back when he annoyed the hell out of her, she'd had no problem finding words. Lots and lots of words.

So that was another symptom. Trouble talking to Luke.

*Could I be in actual love with Luke?* Eve wondered. *Or has the romantic atmosphere, with the stars and the willow tree and the Jess-and-Seth love-fest, gone to my head?*

'Seth!' Jess cried sharply, jerking Eve away from her thoughts. She looked over at him, and her heart pounded. Dots of sweat had appeared on Seth's forehead, and tremors were running through his body. Earlier, she'd thought his eyes looked starry, but now she realized they looked feverish.

'We need to get you to the clinic. My parents are both over there now, Mom doing doctor stuff, and my dad organizing,' Eve said quickly, taking control of the situation.

'Seth's car is right outside,' Jess said, her eyes locked on him.

'He's not OK to drive though,' Luke told her. 'We should—'

Nikolai appeared at the table. 'Everything all right?' he asked. Then he saw Seth. 'I'll call an ambulance,' he said, pulling his cell out of his pocket.

The paramedics arrived in a few minutes, two rolling a gurney, one leading the way. Eve thought maybe they were from the CDC. Whoever they were, they were dressed in hazmat suits. God, those things were scary. The paramedics were probably nice, normal people. But with their faces obscured by the suits' headgear, they could be some kind of alien creatures come to study human beings.

'Let's get you up here,' one of the paramedics told Seth. Even the voice came out sounding inhuman.

'I'm fine to walk,' Seth protested. But he had slumped down in his chair. Eve wasn't sure how long he'd be able to sit up unsupported, forget about walk.

'Seth, let them,' Jess said, her voice sounding thick.

He looked at her, then nodded, allowing the paramedics to help him to the gurney. 'I'm going with him,' Jess called as they began to wheel him across the patio.

'It's not protocol to—' one of the paramedics began.

'I don't care. I'm going with him.' Eve had heard Jess use that tone before – not often, but enough to know that some way, somehow, her friend would, indeed, be going with Seth.

'Jess, we can come too. Or at least meet you there,' Eve said.

'No. Then I'll just be worrying about you guys too,' Jess told them. 'Please just go home and stay safe.'

Luke and Eve exchanged a quick glance, then Luke nodded. 'Call us if you change your mind,' he called after Jess.

Eve flipped over her pillow. The fresh side still felt too warm, and the thin sheet she was using as her only cover felt too heavy, like it was made of lead instead of Egyptian cotton with a very nice thread count.

All she could think about was Seth being wheeled away by the team in their hazmat suits – that and Jess. Jess had kissed Seth so, *so* close to when his symptoms broke out. What if she got sick too? What if she died? Because some of the doctors on the news had predicted fatalities.

Fatalities. Such an icy word. Eve didn't want to think about a world without Jess in it, but now that the thought was in her mind, she couldn't force it out. *Fatalities, fatalities, fatalities.* The word thrummed through her to the beat of her heart.

She couldn't just lie there and take it. She threw off the sheet and jumped out of bed. *Now what?* Standing up hadn't made the horrible thoughts go away. *Hot chocolate*, she decided. Yes, they were in the middle of a crazy heat wave, but hot chocolate had always been her go-to when she was upset. And making it might distract her a teeny, tiny bit.

Eve rushed down the stairs, getting a whiff of that delicious new-clothes smell from her pyjamas. Had she and Jess really been shopping only this afternoon? It felt like a million years ago.

She hurried to the kitchen, flipped on the light, opened the cupboard over the microwave, and pulled out a tin of her favourite Fiori's hot chocolate. Milk next. She opened the fridge and pulled out a carton.

'Hot chocolate. Should have known.'

Eve turned round, startled, and saw Luke standing in the doorway. She gave him a weak smile. 'Couldn't sleep.'

'Yeah, me neither. I heard you going downstairs, so I thought I'd keep you company.'

'Thinking about your dad?' Eve asked. She poured the milk into a saucepan and put it on the stove.

Luke nodded. 'And Seth. And Jess. And everyone, I guess. But mostly them.'

'I'm almost starting to wish there *was* a demon involved,' Eve confessed. 'Just so I could *do* something. Having everything so horrible and just sitting around drinking hot chocolate is going to drive me insane.'

'Like you said, we're going to research, try and find out if there *is* any demon connection. The weather keeps making me think there is. It's too coincidental to have bizarre weather and an epidemic at the same time. It feels supernatural to me,' Luke said. 'Whether it is or not, at least we'll be trying to figure out what's really going on.'

'I keep thinking about Jess and Seth kissing tonight,' Eve told him. 'It was so close to when he got sick. What if she gets sick too?' A cold wave of fear crashed down on her, and she felt tears sting her eyes. She blinked them away, but not fast enough. Luke had seen them. In two long strides he reached her and wrapped her in his arms. He didn't say anything, just held on.

Eve wished she could stop time, at least for a little while, but that was impossible. She didn't want to, but after a long moment, she forced herself to let Luke go. He looked down at her, not stepping away, not releasing her.

He lowered his head, just a little. He was going to kiss her. If she kept standing there staring into his green eyes, he was going to kiss her. And he was a player. And she didn't want to get involved with a player.

She didn't move. Luke brought his lips closer to hers. Eve looped her arms around his neck, and a jolt shot through her body, hot and fizzy. Her power! Before she could stop it, the power jumped from her hand to Luke's neck. He jerked his head back, surprised.

'I'm so sorry!' Eve cried. 'I don't— It just happened.' Emotion had always been a big factor in the control she had over her powers. When she was angry or scared, sometimes . . . *bam!* The power flew free before she released it. But she had never thought that attraction to a guy could have the same effect.

'No worries. It wasn't any worse than sticking a pen in a light socket,' Luke joked gently. 'I did that once when I was ten. It was a forfeit in some game I made up with my friends.'

'Sorry,' Eve said again. 'I should, um, check the milk.' She moved towards the stove, but before she reached it, Luke took her by the shoulders and turned her towards him. 'Hey. It's OK. Really.'

He leaned close, close, closer, and kissed her, soft and gentle. Eve felt it all the way down to her toes, a tingling, sparking sensation that had nothing to do with her power this time. It was all Luke. Maybe this would be a better moment to stop time, Eve thought fuzzily.

Suddenly a high screech cut through the air, shattering the moment. She stumbled away from Luke, whipping her head towards the sound, and saw a grey tabby cat in the tree outside the kitchen window. It stared at her for a split second, its eyes glowing gold in the moonlight, then it leaped from the tree and streaked away.

'A cat!' Eve exclaimed. 'I almost had heart failure and it was just a cat!'

'I'm really not a cat person, at least not any more,' Luke joked.

They looked at each other and both started laughing. Then he stopped laughing and so did she. Eve was pretty sure they were both thinking about their kiss.

'I should probably— We need to get up early to start on the research,' Luke said.

'Yeah. I think I'm just going to go back to bed,' Eve answered. She turned off the stove. 'Not really the time for hot chocolate. The caffeine . . .' They kept looking at each other until Eve turned and started out of the kitchen, Luke following her. *So are we going to pretend it never happened?* Eve wondered. *Or will it be happening again?*

*Luke kissed me!* Eve thought before she even opened her eyes the next morning. She felt a smile take over her face. Or maybe she'd been smiling all night. She had definitely fallen asleep thinking about that kiss, so she'd been smiling then too.

She sat up in bed and yawned in the bright light. It was cool in her bedroom because of the air conditioning, but she could tell just by the colour of the sunlight that today was going to be another scorcher.

*Luke kissed me!* she thought again. *I have to talk to Jess.*

She needed a confab with her best friend to figure out what it meant, that kiss. Was it the start of something? Or just a friendly gesture? The hug had definitely been friendly. But the kiss?

Damn that cat. If it hadn't yowled and broken the mood . . . Actually, Eve wasn't sure what would have happened. But she would have liked the chance to find out. She climbed out of bed. Fuzzy cow slippers or no fuzzy cow slippers? She decided to give the slippers a 'yes'. She loved them – and it was not like they were in any way Care Bear-related.

Now, what about make-up? A little lip gloss before she stepped out of her room, or was that too much? She always thought it was stupid when women in TV shows and movies went to bed with what was clearly a ton of make-up on. If they did that for real, it would be zit city – not to mention the mess it would make of the pillow!

*I'll just fix my hair and maybe use some toner*, she decided as she headed into her bathroom. She had just squirted a blob of leave-in conditioner into her palm when she heard Jess calling her name.

No, not calling. Screaming!

# Chapter Four

Eve flew down the stairs and yanked open the front door, vaguely aware that Luke was a few steps behind her.

'Eve!' Jess screamed again.

'I'm here, I'm right here,' Eve reassured her, shocked by the pallor of her friend's face and the wildness of her eyes.

Luke took Jess by the shoulders. 'You're OK. You're here with us. Take a deep breath and tell us what's wrong.'

Jess gasped, sucking down a lungful of air. 'Seth. I went to see him, and . . . Oh, God, Eve!'

Eve's bones turned to sticks of ice. Had Seth died?

Jess pulled away from Luke and pressed both hands to her mouth, but a sob managed to escape. She shook her head, unable to speak.

'Let's go in the living room. We should all just sit

down,' Eve said. She looped her arm around Jess and started to walk her out of the hall. She looked over at Luke. 'Maybe get her some juice?'

Just as Eve got Jess settled on the sofa, Luke re-appeared with a glass of pomegranate juice. He handed it to Jess and sat down next to her. Eve sat down on her other side and rubbed Jess's back. 'Start again. You went to see Seth, and . . .'

'I almost didn't get to see him. Is my mascara all over my face?' she asked Eve.

Eve knew that wasn't the most important thing on Jess's mind. It's just that whatever had happened was so bad, her friend was having trouble talking about it. 'You look gorgeous, as always,' Eve answered.

'I'm surprised they let you see him at all,' Luke commented. 'They won't let me in to see my dad.'

A small smile tugged at Jess's lips. 'I had to pitch a fit.'

'Jess's fits are legendary. She doesn't go there often, but when she does – look out,' Eve told Luke.

Jess's smile disappeared. 'So, anyway, they said I could see him for a few minutes if I put on one of those hazmat suits, which I did. He's over in the courthouse with a bunch of other sick people because no one else in his family is sick. They have all these cots in the corridors. So many people.'

Her eyes glazed, and Eve could tell Jess was seeing it all again. 'Drink your juice,' she urged.

Jess obediently took a sip. Then another. When she took a third, Eve realized again how hard it was for Jess to talk about whatever had happened to Seth. 'You put on the suit and went to see Seth,' she said, trying to coax Jess back to her story.

Jess nodded. 'Yeah, I saw him. And he was so excited that I came.' She gave another smile, a bigger one, one that looked to Eve like it was about seventy-five per cent real. It faded almost as fast as the last one had.

'It was hard to talk with that suit on. Hard to hear too. It covers your whole head,' Jess continued. Eve struggled to stay patient. They didn't need to know these kinds of details. They needed to know what had freaked Jess out so badly.

'Mostly, we just looked at each other,' Jess said. 'Then . . .' She pulled in a long, shuddering breath. 'Then I saw something on his face. A little dark spot near his chin. I thought it might be a bit of food or something.' Jess's lips began to tremble, but she didn't stop. 'I brushed it away, and his skin came off on my glove.' Her voice got higher with every word. 'It was his skin. That black spot. *Skin.*'

Eve's stomach tightened into a small, hard ball just thinking about it. 'What did the doctors say? You talked to them, right?'

'I screamed until one of them ran over,' Jess answered. 'And the doctor wasn't even shocked. Necrosis, he called it. He said it's a new symptom of Flu X, but that they are keeping that quiet so people won't panic.'

'Everyone is panicked already,' Luke said. 'Did he tell you how many of the plague victims have the necrosis?' Eve noticed that his hands had clenched into fists, his knuckles white from the strain.

'They would have told you if your dad had it,' Eve reassured him.

'She just said that they're keeping it quiet,' Luke snapped. He shoved his hair away from his face. 'Sorry.'

Eve reached across Jess and touched Luke's hand. 'It's OK. If my dad— It's OK, Luke.'

Jess swallowed hard. 'There were more splotches of it on Seth's body. On his shoulder. On his neck. One of his feet was almost entirely black. I couldn't even . . . I didn't . . . I just turned round and ran. I ran,

Eve. Seth is going to hate me! I acted like he was repulsive.'

'He'll understand,' Luke told her. 'The guy is crazy about you.'

'Those spots, they're so horrible. It's like the people who get them are dying piece by piece, their flesh just . . . sliding off the bones,' Jess said. 'Seeing it, I think it has to be a demon thing. It's so awful, it has to be.'

'I think so too,' Eve answered.

Luke nodded.

'I don't get how it got in though,' Eve said. 'The portal is blocked.'

'Maybe that's one of the things we should research,' Luke suggested. 'We should get started as soon as possible.'

'I don't think I'm going to be able to focus on anything but Seth,' Jess admitted. 'Maybe you two should just do the research without me.'

'No,' Eve said firmly. 'We need you, Jess. We have to figure this thing out as fast as possible. It's the best thing you can do for Seth, and besides, it will give you something to do other than worry.'

'You're right. So let's meet up at my house after school and get to it. Seth might call on my home phone instead of the cell, and I don't want to miss him.' Eve could tell Jess was struggling to keep her voice bright and peppy. 'I have to get home and change.' She stood up.

Eve walked Jess to the front door. She gave her a hard hug. 'See you at school.' As Jess stepped outside, she caught sight of Mrs Brownlee across the street. She was wearing plastic gloves and a safety mask as she hauled overflowing bags of groceries up the driveway.

Eve noticed that the bags were from a store over in East Hampton. Could the Deepdene store be completely sold out? Had the panic buying gotten that bad?

She shut the door, overwhelmed by the feeling that things in Deepdene were getting worse by the second. *Jess, Luke, and I have already saved the town twice,* she thought. *We can do it again.*

'This is just spooky,' Jess murmured as she and Eve walked into the cafeteria for lunch a few hours later.

'Spreepy,' Eve agreed, the word for spooky-plus-creepy that they'd come up with back in third grade.

For starters, the caf was way too quiet. Everyone was talking in whispers. None of the guys were up to their usual shenanigans designed to get the girls to look at them. Sometimes Eve was amazed by boys. Did they really think getting a girl to notice them while they were doing something inane – like shot-gunning a soda – was a good thing?

The caf was also way too empty, just like every one of Eve's morning classes had been. 'How many people do you think are absent today?' Eve whispered. There wasn't a reason to whisper, except that everyone else was. But it felt wrong to speak at a normal volume when the big room was so silent.

'I don't know,' Jess whispered back as they got in line – if you could call three people a line – at the lunch counter. 'In art, it was almost half the class. But it wasn't as bad in the other periods.'

'I heard James Frankel's family actually left town,' Katy Emory said from her spot in front of Jess. She spoke in a normal tone, and it almost sounded like she was shouting. 'He's skiing in Aspen right now.'

'Briony's parents must be relieved that she took off to see her old boyfriend,' Eve commented. 'I bet they told her not to come back until after there's a vaccine or antibiotics you can take.'

'The Frankels probably got extra-freaked living next door to the Delawares,' Jess commented, voice still low. She took a yogurt, put it on her tray, then moved the tray a little further down the metal rails. 'Belinda was one of the first people to get sick, remember? And her brother got it a couple of days later.'

'Oh, God, did you hear the latest about Belinda?' Katy asked, this time bringing her voice down too. 'There's a rumour going around that pieces of her *face* are falling off. Shanna was telling me that her parents brought in this plastic surgeon to the stars from LA to see what he could do for her.' Katy gently patted her cheeks as if to make sure the skin was still there. 'Belinda was supposedly completely losing it every time she looked in the mirror.'

'Who wouldn't be?' Jess asked.

'True,' Katy said. 'I wish there was something we could do for them, for everybody. But signing a card or something like that seems almost pathetic, with everything so horrible.'

'We should do it anyway,' Eve said. She realized she was almost at the cash register and hadn't chosen any food. She grabbed a turkey sandwich, an apple and a soda. She had to make sure she kept herself in top form. Fighting a demon while coping with a hunger headache was probably a bad idea.

'See you guys later,' Katy said after she'd paid. She

headed off for a table by the windows, where Tim Bentley was clearly waiting for her.

'Do you want to hear some non-plague-related gossip?' Eve asked after she paid for her food. 'But before we go sit with everybody.'

'God, yes,' Jess said.

'It's about Luke,' Eve told her. 'And me,' she added as they loitered near the condiment counter so they could have some privacy.

Jess raised her eyes. 'Well, don't stop now.'

'He kissed me.' The words weren't nearly good enough to express the actual experience.

Jess clearly didn't think so either. 'I need many more details than that. When? Where? What were you wearing?'

'Last night – late. My kitchen. My new pyjamas,' Eve answered.

'I knew those were a good purchase,' Jess said. 'Go on.'

'I was upset about . . . everything.' She wasn't going to tell Jess she'd been freaking over the idea that Jess could have contracted the plague from kissing Seth. 'And Luke hugged me. A friend, comfort hug. But then, all of a sudden, it just changed and we were kissing.'

'And then what?' Jess demanded.

'And then nothing,' Eve said. 'A cat let out this horrible yowl, and we jumped apart, and then—' She shrugged.

'You guys remembered that for some ridiculous reason you should be friends and friends only,' Jess said.

'I guess,' Eve agreed. Maybe her reasons for not wanting to get involved with Luke were ridiculous. Maybe he was only a player because he hadn't found a girl he wanted to hang with all the time. Maybe she was that girl. Maybe – but this wasn't the time to be thinking about it. 'Let's go eat.'

People weren't sitting in their usual groups and tables. Too many kids were gone for that. Eve and Jess walked over to the table where Rose, Dave, Phoebe and Bet were eating. Eve didn't think she'd ever shared a lunch table with Dave Perry or Phoebe Abbott. Not for any real reason. They just hung with different groups. A glance out of the window showed her that Luke and a couple of other guys were eating out on the lawn.

'You heard about Jenna already, right?' Rose asked as they sat down.

'Jenna's sick?' Eve cried. From the expression on Rose's face, it couldn't be anything else.

'Didn't even make it through homeroom,' Rose replied. 'Sweat popped out all over her forehead and she started to slide out of her chair. It was awful. Ms Fraser asked for volunteers to help her to the office, and for a minute nobody moved. And you know how usually everyone jumps up if there's a chance to get out of class.'

'Everybody's scared,' Jess said.

'Yeah. Yeah,' Rose repeated, as if there was nothing more that could even be said. 'I'll be back in a minute. I just need to get something from my locker. Watch my stuff, OK?'

'Sure,' Eve told her.

'How many of them do you think there are now? Sick people from school, I mean,' Phoebe asked.

Eve suddenly wished she had her safety mask on. She'd worn it in the classes where people were sitting close to her, but it wasn't like she could keep it on and eat.

'Look around,' Dave said to Phoebe, using his fork to gesture at the empty tables around them. 'I heard that they're going to close the school today. Not enough teachers. Not enough kids.'

*More time to research. That would be good,* Eve thought. And who could concentrate anyway, with so many of their friends sick?

'I heard the CDC is going to *order* the school closed,' Bet added. 'Too dangerous to have this many people congregating.'

'Do you think it's because of the way the disease is going?' Dave asked. 'You guys heard that people with it have rotting skin now, right? It turns all black and then falls off.'

'What?' Bet exclaimed. 'WHAT?'

'It's a new symptom,' Jess explained. She frowned, 'Seth . . . Seth actually has it. The skin really does slide off, no exaggeration.'

'That's so horrible!' Bet cried. 'They're never going to be the same, even if somebody figures out a cure. After the skin thing, they'll all have horrible scars, won't they?'

'I couldn't handle that,' Phoebe told them. 'Maybe that's shallow, but I couldn't.' She ran her hands up and down her arms. 'I'm all itchy now. I want to leave and go lock myself in my closet until this is over.'

'There's a janitor over there,' Eve said. She didn't recognize the man, but there'd been some new people around, filling in for plague victims. 'I'm going to ask him if the school is really closing today.'

'I'm coming,' Phoebe said. 'If it's not closing, I'm just going to ditch. Suddenly I feel like the air in here is disgusting. I don't want it in me. Way too many people from school are sick.' She and Eve stood up.

Jess did too. 'Watch Rose's stuff, OK?' she asked Dave and Bet.

'Will do,' Bet answered as Eve and the others started towards the janitor.

Eve hesitated, then turned round. 'If school is closed, come over to my house tomorrow if you want. Around three. We can hang by the pool where there's fresh air,' she said impulsively. 'Tell people.' She knew her mom would be annoyed at her for getting a group together when they could so easily be passing this plague around, but they were all in this together. Some people might not want to be alone. She didn't.

'Cool,' Dave said.

Eve, Jess and Phoebe hurried over to the janitor. 'Um, excuse me,' Eve said. 'We were just wondering if you know whether or not they're closing the school today?'

The man just gave a little grunt, not bothering to look up from his mopping. 'Hey!' Jess protested and he slopped the mop over her Stella McCartney sandals. The janitor didn't apologize. Instead, he lumbered away, dragging the mop awkwardly behind him.

'Let's go to the office and ask.' Jess rolled her eyes. 'That guy is clearly useless.'

'Good idea,' Eve answered.

The school secretary looked wary as the three of them walked into the office. 'Ms K, you always know the scoop,' Jess said, putting both hands on the counter. 'Is school closing today?'

'I'm getting asked the question again,' Ms Keener called towards the principal's open door.

A few seconds later, Ms Allison stepped out, looking like she hadn't slept in for ever. 'I'm going to make the announcement right now. No classes after lunch. No school until further notice.'

'You girls go get your things together,' Ms Keener said. 'I can't believe it's come to this.'

'Luke beat us here,' Jess said as she and Eve turned down their street and saw him waiting outside Eve's house.

'Figured it would be easier to just come here with the madness at school,' Luke explained as they reached him. 'I didn't see you two at your lockers.'

'Good call,' Eve told him.

The school had been crazed as soon as the

principal's announcement had come over the inter-com. Pretty much everyone had heard the rumours that the school was going to close, but the fact that it was actually happening seemed to make some people realize how truly scary the situation was in the town. Somehow, going to school every day had made things seem a little normal, a little safe.

Some people tried to stuff every single thing they had accumulated in their lockers into one backpack, although, really, none of it was necessary. There'd been crying and hugging. Regina Fortes fainted in the hall. Everyone – including Regina – thought she was the latest plague victim, but she'd been having a panic attack.

Jess unlocked her front door and ushered them in. They headed through to the kitchen and for a few minutes they occupied themselves choosing drinks and snacks. It was a tiny little piece of ordinary, and Eve appreciated it. 'Any ideas on what to research?' she asked when she had picked out a can of Hansen's Tangerine Green Tea.

'Plagues and freak high temperatures at the same time,' Luke suggested.

'Demons that cause plagues,' Jess said.

'Not so much to go on,' Eve commented. She

looked over at Luke. 'You think it's time, don't you?'

'I think we might find the info we need if we ask the Order for help,' Luke answered.

'OK, let's call Callum,' Eve said. Callum was a high-level member of the Order. They'd met him when he came to Deepdene to retrieve Payne's body. Eve had told him the truth about herself, about her powers, about being the current Deepdene Witch. Payne had told his superior parts of her story anyway. Eve thought the Order might as well know the rest.

'It'll be faster if I just call Alanna. She's lower level. She'll be easier to get in touch with than Callum.' Luke pulled out his cell. 'I'll put her on speaker.'

'Wait. You have Alanna's phone number?' Eve asked. Alanna was a twenty-something member of the Order, a protégée of Payne's. She'd come with Callum to Deepdene, and while she was there she'd made it clear she didn't like Eve. 'The card Callum gave us didn't have her contact info on it.'

'She called me once,' Luke said, suddenly seeming very interested in the bowl of trail mix in front of him. 'To see if we were having any more problems.'

'Huh.' Eve was not going to ask Luke why he hadn't told her about the call. She'd sound like a jealous girlfriend, and she and Luke were so not a couple. They'd kissed one time. That was it.

'So. Alanna?' Luke asked.

'Go ahead. Faster is better,' Eve said. She thought she'd managed to keep the irritation out of her voice. She couldn't stop herself from watching him use the cell though. He didn't have Alanna on speed dial. That was something.

'Luke, hey, good to hear from you,' Alanna said. 'How're you doing?' She was one of those girls who sounded like she was flirting no matter what she said. She shouldn't be flirting with Luke. She was way too old for him.

'Not that great,' Luke answered. 'That's why I'm calling. We think we might have another demon situation in Deepdene.'

'We've been following the extreme temperatures you've been having and the outbreak of Flu X. We haven't found anything to indicate demon involvement,' Alanna answered.

'Nice of you to tell us that. Finally,' Eve snapped. She shot an outraged glance at Jess, who looked almost as angry as Eve felt.

'Oh, I'm on speaker,' Alanna said. 'I thought this was a private conversation, Luke.'

'Eve and Jess are here too,' Luke told her. 'We—'

'I'm definitely here,' Eve cut in. 'We live in this town, remember. And we're the ones who told you about the portal. You demon experts didn't even know about it. As soon as you decided to investigate, you should have called me.'

'You're the demon hunter,' Alanna shot back. 'You can even smell them, as I remember. I wouldn't think you'd need our help detecting demonic presence.'

Eve suspected Alanna was jealous of her ability to kill demons without one of the special swords. That made her feel a little better.

'We want to do some research anyway. We all believe there's a demon here,' Luke said. 'If you come across anything we can use as a starting place, will you let us know?'

'If you're nice,' Alanna replied.

'When am I not nice?' he asked.

Was he flirting back? He'd kind of flirted with Alanna when she was here. But, come on, she was *waaay* too old.

'Luke's always nice. To everyone,' Jess said pointedly, getting Eve's back.

'Absolutely everyone. You're nothing special,' Eve added. Luke raised an eyebrow at her and she gave an

apologetic shrug. That hadn't been exactly necessary
– or nice. But she'd enjoyed it.

'So you'll call, right?' Jess asked. She tapped her
fingers on the kitchen table.

'I'll call you, Luke,' Alanna said, with just a touch of
emphasis on the 'you'.

Luke said goodbye and hung up.

'Well, that was helpful.' Jess took a sip of her soda.

'Infuriating,' Eve agreed. 'I cannot believe she didn't
contact us. Or any of the Order.' She turned to Luke.
'Can you?'

'Definitely not cool,' he answered. He tilted his head
from side to side, cracking his neck. 'So I guess we go
online and start researching demons, and plagues and
heat waves.'

'Oh, my!' Jess said. They all laughed at her *Wizard
of Oz* joke, even though it wasn't that funny. Laughing
felt like it sucked some of the stress out of Eve's body.

'Sounds good to—'

Eve was interrupted by Jess's brother Peter,
barrelling into the room. 'We're going on lockdown.'
He grabbed an enormous handful of trail mix and
stuffed it into his mouth.

'I want to say "what?"' Jess said. 'But I don't want to
see you talk with your mouth full.'

Peter opened his mouth as wide as possible and gave them all a good look. Eve could have predicted that move. She'd known Peter for ever – he was basically her surrogate little brother.

'OK, so the whole town is going into lockdown,' Peter said after he'd swallowed, with the aid of a swig from Luke's soda. 'Starting at ten o'clock, no one is getting in or out.'

'That can't be right,' Luke told him. 'It's completely unconstitutional for one thing.'

'If you say so, but look.' Peter flipped on the TV and there was the WELCOME TO DEEPDENE sign, and next to it a small booth with a guard inside – a guard in a hazmat suit. The image changed to an aerial view showing a five-metre wire fence being erected around the whole town. The workers erecting the fence were all wearing hazmat suits too.

Luke swore softly under his breath. 'It's like we're watching one of those post-apocalyptic movies.'

Peter didn't say anything. Not typical. Although he was the one who'd told them the news, Eve thought actually seeing Deepdene being locked down had hit him hard.

'It went by too fast, but I think that guard had a

rifle.' Jess's eyes were wide. 'Are they actually going to shoot people who try to leave?'

A terrifying thought exploded in Eve's brain. 'No one can leave,' she said. She looked at Luke and Jess. They didn't get it yet. 'No one can leave,' she repeated, and the horror on Luke and Jess's faces made it clear that this time they understood. If their suspicions were correct, they were trapped in their little town – with a demon.

'I just thought of something else. It didn't hit me until now,' Luke said as Jess powered up her laptop a little later that afternoon. She'd positioned it in the middle of her bed so she, Luke, and Eve could all see it. 'The Order won't be able to send anyone in if we need them. There's no way for them to get in with the guards and the fences.'

'We don't need Alanna or the Order,' Eve assured him. 'We just need us – you, me and Jess. The three of us have taken on demons alone before.'

Luke didn't remind her that Payne had sacrificed his life when they were battling the wargs together. He wasn't sure any of them would have lived through that night without the Order.

'I just put in *plague* and *demon* and got many, many, many hits,' Jess told them.

Luke checked the screen. She wasn't kidding. 'Try doing *heatwave* with those two,' he suggested. His cell buzzed as Jess added the word to the search. He checked it, and relief swept over him like a cool breeze. 'Text from Callum. He says he's sent me an email. Maybe the Order found something useful.'

'They have been incredibly helpful so far,' Eve snarked. Luke agreed that the Order should have told them they were looking into the strange happenings in Deepdene. But he was sure they would have if they'd uncovered anything. Probably Alanna and the others didn't want to call to say they had nothing to say. That wouldn't have been incredibly helpful either.

Jess turned the laptop towards him and Luke quickly logged on to his gmail account. He clicked on Callum's message. 'He sent us a link,' Luke told the girls. 'He says it might be useful, but he's dubious.'

'I can just hear him saying that. "Dubious" is a Callum kind of word,' Jess commented.

'What's the link to?' Eve asked.

'An article on an ancient Egyptian papyrus scroll from some university I've never heard of.' Luke began to skim the article. Eve and Jess moved in closer so they could read it too.

Briefly, Luke was distracted by a whiff of fragrance from Eve. A mix of coconut and sunshine. A mix of suntan lotion and *her*. It made him want to kiss her again.

Man, why had he let a cat screw things up between them? A *cat*. But the kiss had happened so spontaneously. And after the cat, there was just too much time to think, to wonder if Eve had wanted him to kiss her in the first place. She'd certainly bolted out of the kitchen pretty fast. Not that he hadn't. He—

'Demon!' Jess exclaimed, returning Luke to the subject he should have been thinking about all along. She pointed to the word near the bottom of the first page. Clearly she'd been skimming too.

'*The warning on the scroll is believed to refer to a demon often called Many Faces but sometimes referred to as Amunnic*,' Luke read. '*The demon lives by drinking human blood*.'

'Back up,' Eve said. 'What warning are they talking about?'

'Back up,' Jess said. 'The thing drinks *blood*?'

'That's what it said. Blood,' Luke answered. 'There's a translation of the scroll and one of the lines says "Ye shall know him by the coming of the plague". That has to be the warning.'

'Sounds like a warning to me,' Jess said.

'So this Many Faces or Amunnic brings a plague, is that what it's saying?' Eve asked. 'That sounds sort of like Malphas. He brought bad dreams to weaken his victims with lack of sleep. That way, it was easier to feed on them. Maybe Many Faces wants weak victims too and that's what the plague does.'

*My dad*, Luke thought. *A demon could be preparing my father so it can feed on him. All the others too.* His gut began to churn. His dad was a minister. If he knew he was giving a demon strength that would horrify him more than dying from the plague. 'Now that we have a name, let's see what else we can find out.'

Jess did a search for Amunnic and Many Faces. Only three hits came up. 'I hope one of them says why he's called Many Faces – that's freaky.'

Eve laughed.

'What?' Jess asked as she clicked the first hit.

'So much is freaky, it's like freaky is normal,' she explained. She laughed again. 'I know it's not that funny. I'm just stressed.'

'Wimp,' Luke teased, smiling at her.

'This one just mentions Amunnic–slash–Many

Faces in a list of demons. No other info,' Jess said. 'Moving on. Another list of demons, but we get a few more details. Sightings in ancient Egypt, which we knew because of the scroll.'

'Doh.' Luke slapped his forehead. He couldn't believe he hadn't instantly made the connection. 'Egypt! Where Mr Dokey was!'

'So maybe he *did* bring back the plague!' Eve exclaimed. 'Not as a virus or some kind of bug. He somehow brought the demon to Deepdene.'

'That would explain why the portal was still closed,' Jess said. 'This demon didn't come through the portal. Eve, maybe that's why you haven't been smelling anything demony – maybe that wood-smoke smell comes from the portal, whenever a demon passes through it.'

'Isn't it bad enough we have a doorway to hell,' Luke asked, rubbing his face with both hands, 'without demons choosing Deepdene as some kind of vacation spot?'

'I guess the travel brochures didn't mention that Deepdene has its own demon-fighting witch,' Eve joked. 'A witch with a whole team to back her up.' She looked back and forth between Luke and Jess. 'I love you guys, you know,' she added, turning serious.

'We love you too.' Jess reached out and gave her a half-hug.

'Yeah,' Luke said. And he did love her as a friend. But he was really starting to think he might *love* her too. *Don't lose your focus*, he told himself. His dad needed him sharp. The whole town did. 'What else does the entry say?' Luke asked Jess.

'Oh. Not good.' Jess frowned at the computer screen. '*The demon is also known as Many Faces for its ability to take on the appearance of any human or animal it chooses.*'

There was a long stretch of silence as they all took in the implications. 'So it could be anybody,' Eve said. 'Or at least it could look like anybody. As many any-bodys as it wanted to, sounds like.'

There was a scratching sound on Jess's door, and Luke started a little. *On edge, much?* he asked himself.

'It's just Ringo,' Jess told them. 'He scratches when he wants in.' She stood up and let in her poodle. When Jess sat back down on the bed, Ringo joined her, nosing Eve and Luke, tail wagging furiously.

'It could even be Ringo,' Eve said. She'd been scratching the poodle's stomach and she slowly moved her hand away.

Jess cradled Ringo to her. 'It could so not be my

sweetums,' she answered, burying her face in his curly hair. 'I mean it could be,' she added, 'but it's not.'

'Probably not,' Luke agreed. 'But from here on out, we've got to be in trust-no-one mode.'

'Anything else on that page?' Eve asked.

'Nope,' Jess answered. Her fingers flew across the keyboard. 'And the next entry is just a list of demon names. What next?'

'How about that line from the scroll? The one about knowing him from the coming of the plague,' Luke suggested. 'Maybe cut and paste the line in Arabic. That should narrow things down a little.'

'On it,' Jess said.

Luke noticed that Eve had returned to petting Ringo, but her sapphire-blue eyes looked even darker than usual.

'Mmm. Here's something about the translation,' Jess said. 'It says that the line is often misinterpreted. What it really means is that a plague arrives before the demon, not that the demon brings the plague.'

'Huh.' Luke drew his eyebrows together. 'Like some kind of demon alarm?'

'It was a curse,' Eve announced. She pointed to the footnote she'd spotted. 'It says that Amunnic wasn't always preceded by the plague. The plague was a curse put on the demon by an Egyptian priest. He wanted to give people a warning that a demon was among them. The curse sent a plague before the demon – a plague and a heatwave – arriving in each place the demon went, to give the people there a warning that a demon was among them.'

Jess frowned. 'So you mean that the plague isn't the badness. The plague is just an *announcement* of the badness?'

'It seems like the priest just gave them something else to worry about in addition to the demon,' Luke said. He didn't get it.

'Yeah, couldn't the priest have made, I don't know, rainbows appear when the demon was close? Why make people sick to tell them there's a demon? That just seems mean.'

'Maybe curses aren't that easy to perform,' Eve suggested. 'Maybe that was the best he could do. Any power has limitations.' Luke was pretty sure she was thinking about her own power.

'Yeah, that's why you've been able to bring down the other demons. Their power has limitations,' Luke told her, choosing to misunderstand.

Eve reached out and put her hand over one of Luke's. 'This is good news for your dad, I think. Good news for everyone who has the plague. Once we kill the demon, they'll all be OK again. No demon, no need for demon-warning system.'

Luke wasn't entirely sure that logic made sense. Yeah, no demon, no need for demon-warning system. But maybe that just meant no new people would get the plague and not that the people who already had it would be cured.

'I can't stop thinking about the part where it feeds on blood,' Jess admitted. 'I just found some more on that. Listen. It says before the curse, the demon could destroy entire communities in days.' She took a sharp intake of breath as she read on. 'There was one village – I can't pronounce the name – where in just a few days, every single person was completely drained of blood.'

# Chapter Five

Eve opened the sliding door to the back patio, a fresh pitcher of berry and lime smoothie in one hand. She was glad she'd told people to come over today. With so many of her friends sick, it felt good to have some of the others close around her, and she thought they felt the same way. Most people had arrived around three, and it was now nearly six.

Not that any of them were able to completely enjoy the impromptu party. The behaviour seemed to fall into three general groups. There were the people like Dave and Megan, who were acting exaggeratedly happy, straining to have fun, fun, fun – so much fun they couldn't think. It was easy to see the panic underneath. Jess's little brother Peter was in this group too. He'd invited himself to the party even though he wasn't even in high school yet, and had been cannonballing into the pool almost non-stop. He'd arrived to tell her Jess would be showing up late, and had never left.

Then there were the people who were huddled in little groups, like Katy and Alexander, talking about the plague – and only the plague – expressions tight and anxious.

And, finally, there were a couple of people who were staying off by themselves, lost in their own thoughts, so much so they probably hardly realized they were even at a party. Luke was in this group, thinking about his dad, maybe, or about how anyone poolside at Eve's right this moment could be a demon in disguise, or maybe about how they'd been researching all morning and hadn't turned up any new information about Amunnic.

Eve set the pitcher on one of the patio tables, and walked towards Luke. 'Do you think she'll ever be actually pretty again? Or does the skin just never come back?' she heard Bet asking Katy and Alexander.

She picked up her speed, not wanting to hear the answer. When she reached Luke, she sat down on the end of his lounger. 'Hi.'

It took him a moment to say 'Hi' back. He'd been far away in his thoughts.

'I should be wearing my mask,' Eve admitted. 'But

my mom isn't home, and how can you have a party with a reminder of the plague walking around? Not that half the people aren't talking about the plague anyway. And the new curfew.' In addition to the lock-down, a nine-o'clock curfew was now in place, so that it was easier to account for the whereabouts of Deepdene residents at night.

'They aren't even sure masks can stop the plague from spreading,' Luke answered. 'And now we know that what we're trying to stop isn't really the disease at all. You know.' He clearly didn't want to say the word 'demon' with all the people milling around. Good call.

'Eve, Luke! Get in here!' Megan cried from the shallow end of the pool. She was perched on Dave's shoulders. 'We challenge you to a chicken fight! I knock Eve off your shoulders, and we win. She knocks me off, you two win. And so you know, I rock at this.'

'Maybe later,' Eve called back.

*At least Megan isn't sick*, Eve thought. Jess's next-door neighbour had been put in a psychiatric hospital after a demon attack just a few months ago. She didn't deserve to be a demon victim again. Not that anyone deserved any of this.

'You didn't ask if I wanted to chicken fight,' Luke commented. He sat up and took off his sunglasses, and Eve felt as if he'd returned to her from the dark place his thoughts had taken him.

'*Did* you want to?' she asked. And suddenly she was thinking about their kiss. Again. What was he—

'I've arrived!' Jess called from the side gate.

'Me too!' Bet rushed up behind her. 'Is Rose here?' she called out as they came into the back yard.

'Rose hasn't come, at least not yet,' Eve called back.

'I still have her purse,' Bet said when Eve reached her and Jess. 'She never came back for it yesterday.'

'Maybe she just forgot it when the announcement was made about school closing,' Eve suggested. 'Everyone was running around like crazy.'

'Nobody forgets a Valentino bag,' Jess said. 'Especially not the purple patent leather one with the bow detail.'

Eve and Bet nodded, and Eve felt the smoothie she'd had earlier begin to curdle in her stomach. 'Do you think she got sick?' She didn't want to use the plague word about Rose.

'Yikes. I hope not,' Bet answered. 'I'm going to ask around. Maybe someone's seen her since then.'

'OK, let's have it. What's your excuse for being late to my party?' Eve asked Jess. 'The best-friend code says the best friend shall be the first to arrive and the

106

last to leave, so as to be available to offer any assistance the other best friend might need.'

'I told Peter to tell you I'd be a little late,' Jess said. Like that was an actual answer.

Eve raised an eyebrow. 'Are you really attempting to not tell what you were doing?'

'Did you make berry and lime smoothies?' Jess asked, looking over Eve's shoulder at the pitcher. 'Yum. I'm going to get one.'

Eve put her hand on Jess's arm, stopping her. She stared into Jess's face. 'I'm waiting,' she announced.

It only took a few seconds for her to crack. They were best friends. No secrets allowed. Another part of the code. 'I went to a martial arts class,' Jess burst out.

'That's so cool! Why wouldn't you want to tell me that?' Eve asked.

Jess lowered her voice, aware of the other people around them. 'I guess I was starting to feel like the weak link in our little group,' she confessed. 'I signed up because I wanted a superpower of my own. You have your witch stuff, and Luke has the magic sword that can kill demons.'

'You *are* always standing around texting while Luke and I risk our lives,' Eve joked. But Jess didn't laugh. Eve studied her friend's face. Jess was serious. She really felt like she didn't contribute. 'Jess, come on. You were as much a part of rescuing Vic from the hell-hounds as any of us. And you came up with the idea for how I might be able to close the portal. You aren't the weak anything.'

'This new demon really scares me,' Jess confessed. 'Really, really. I couldn't even let Ringo sleep on my bed last night. That's how freaked I got. I kept think-ing how Many Faces could be anywhere.' She forced a smile. 'But now that I'm learning kung fu, I'll be unstoppable. And I'll have the best butt in school. Those moves really work the glutes.'

'I think I should come with you next time,' Eve said. 'I'm surprised they're even having classes with the town in lockdown and everything.'

'There were only two other people,' Jess said. 'But the instructor, Master Justin, says that the discipline of kung fu isn't something that should ever be abandoned. He said at a time of crisis you need the centring it gives you even more, and that's why he's still giving classes.'

'You may have your smoothie now,' Eve told Jess. 'And there's a bunch of food on the kitchen table. Go and—'

'Hey, guys!' Alexander called from the other side of

the pool. 'Leo Mackenzie got shut out of town last night. My brother just called to tell me. He was in Amagansett for a gig with his band and didn't make it home before the lockdown.'

'Wouldn't they just have let him in if he got home late?' Dave asked as he climbed out of the pool. 'Like check his ID or something?'

'I don't think any exceptions are going to be made,' Luke said.

'I have his cell number,' Megan said. 'I'm calling him.' She got out of the pool and hurried over to the lounger where she'd left her bag. Everyone at the party watched as she tried to reach Leo. 'Went directly to voicemail. And it's full. I couldn't even leave a message.'

'His parents couldn't get through to him either,' Alexander said.

'How long do you think it'll be before he can get back in?' Bet asked.

'They're working on an antibiotic for the plague, according to my mom,' Eve said. 'A vaccine too. Hopefully it won't be too long.'

'Lucky Briony. *Forced* to stay with her boyfriend the whole time we're locked in,' Katy commented.

'You didn't hear?' Megan asked. 'Briony never

showed at the boyfriend's. Her father thought that's where she'd go, but her mom told my mom that she didn't. She hasn't called or anything.'

Eve felt like crushed ice was sliding through her veins. Rose still wasn't here. She'd vanished from school without her stuff. Rose and Briony were both missing. And Leo would have gotten in touch with *somebody* if he'd been locked out, surely. Phones and the internet were still up and running.

'Come help me in the kitchen a minute,' she said to Jess. Luke was already heading towards them from the other side of the patio, face grim. Eve gestured for him to follow them inside.

'This can't be a coincidence,' Eve said the moment the three of them were alone. 'Three people missing. No one's heard from them. That has to be because of Amunnic.'

'Who is Leo, anyway?' Luke asked.

'A guy from the neighbourhood. He graduated last year,' Eve said. 'He's kind of been what his parents like to call a late bloomer. He didn't go to college. All he cares about is guitar.'

Jess sat down in one of the kitchen chairs so suddenly it was as if her legs had gone boneless. 'Amunnic is drinking his blood. Rose and Briony's too.' Her voice cracked as she said the words.

'We don't know that for sure,' Luke said, then he sighed. 'But Amunnic is here. So I guess we pretty much do know it.'

'If he's got Leo, he must have grabbed him before he even got out of town yesterday,' Eve said. 'Amunnic has to have Rose, Briony and Leo somewhere in town.' *Or at least their bodies.* She couldn't stop that hideous thought from slamming into her brain. 'We just have to figure out where.'

'Somewhere with no people,' Jess said. She kicked off her sandals.

'Is it helping?' Eve asked, nodding towards Jess's shoes.

'Not yet,' Jess said.

'Jess has this thing where she believes she thinks better when she's barefoot,' Eve explained to Luke.

'Good thing my shoes are already off,' Luke answered. 'OK, somewhere with no people around . . . Let me use your iPhone,' he said to Jess. 'My cell gets to the internet with the speed of a toddler on a tricycle.' Jess took it out of her tote and handed it to him. 'I'm going to look at some maps to help us come up with places.'

'Deepdene's just not that big,' Eve said.

'And there aren't many empty buildings,' Jess agreed. 'The whole town is what Megan's mom calls real-estate platinum.'

'It looks like there's a big building out beyond the railway station. You two have any idea what it is?' Luke asked, peering at a satellite map on the iPhone.

'By the station? I can't think of anything out there.' Jess wiggled.

'Oh, wait!' Eve exclaimed. 'It's the power plant! Remember, Jess? We took a tour of it in Mrs Gleeson's fifth-grade class.'

'I think we have our possible evil lair,' Jess said, sliding her sandals back on.

'It's a working plant?' Luke asked.

'Not really. They shut almost all of it down about two years ago,' Eve replied. 'They opened this big plant out in Montauk to handle the entire district, and the Deepdene one is supposed to be used only as backup in case of an overload to the system. It's really old, so I guess it wasn't efficient enough to be the main plant any more.'

'And the county is pretty bad about keeping it up, because of money,' Jess said. 'My mom is talking about starting a campaign to make them get rid of the place entirely since it's an eyesore, all overgrown and stuff. There's nobody ever there except maybe a security guard, maybe not even that with the plague. The thing is barely even functioning.'

'Power plant it is, then.' Luke stood up.

'Jess, how about you go tell people my mom's coming home early because she's not feeling that well. We need to end this party fast,' Eve said.

'That should do it,' Jess said, starting for the door.

Luke looked at Eve. 'I think it's time for Amunnic to leave town.'

The good thing about Deepdene was that nothing was all that far from anything else. It only took Eve, Jess and Luke about twenty minutes to walk-and-jog to the plant. Against the darkening sky, Eve could see the even-darker towers of the power plant.

The thing might barely even be on, but it still gave off a hum that sent tingles through Eve's fingers.

Luke looked over at Jess. 'What do you think, kung-fu chick? One or two karate chops to take it down?' The fence was about three metres high, made of wire mesh and metal bars.

Jess stuck her tongue out at him, then turned and started climbing. Eve followed her. When she reached the top, Eve hung onto the metal bar, swung her body over and let herself hang from her arms. It had seemed like a good plan at the time. But when she twisted her head and looked over her shoulder, the ground seemed a lot further away than she expected. She wasn't used to jumping off pyramids of people the way her cheerleader best friend was.

'You can do it, Evie!' Jess called softly.

Well, she was going to, whether she could or not. Her upper-body strength wasn't all that good, and her arms were already starting to ache. Eve took a deep breath, then let go. She stumbled when she landed, but managed to stay on her feet. A few seconds later, Luke dropped down onto the ground beside her.

'I could see the guard house from the top of the fence. But it looked dark – he's probably down with the plague,' he said, nodding towards the far side of the plant, where a drive led into the small parking lot. 'Still, we should try and get in on the side that doesn't have a guard house, just to be safe.'

'Nice work. You clearly picked up some skills from all those Hardy Boys books. We saw them in your room, you know,' Eve added to Luke, then winked at Jess.

'Don't knock my boys. Although, just so you know, I don't read them any more,' Luke said as they circled around to the side of the big building farthest from the parking lot. He made a 'down' motion with one hand when they got close to a row of windows.

Eve crouch-walked over to the nearest one and peered inside. 'No demon in there,' she told Jess and Luke. They stayed low as they headed for the door, just in case.

'Now what?' Jess asked after she gave the knob an experimental twist and found it locked. 'I haven't gotten to the kung-fu lesson about breaking through doors.'

'Lucky for us, this door takes credit cards,' Luke said. 'Guess they aren't that worried about security if you can trip the lock that way. Do you think there's an alarm?'

Eve snorted. 'They won't even pay for a weed wacker,' she said, kicking at one of the dandelions that sprouted up from between the cracks in the pavement. 'They're definitely not paying for an alarm service.'

'Does the credit card thing even work? It does sound like something that would only work in those books you never read any more,' Jess said.

'OK, who has a card they don't care if I mess up?' Luke asked.

Eve and Jess looked at each other. 'Why don't you mess up one of yours?' Eve finally asked.

Luke laughed. 'Cause, unlike you two princesses, I don't have one.'

'I'm not giving the AmEx,' Eve said.

'Me neither,' Jess answered. 'Who knows if my parents would ever get me another one. They're always threatening to take it away.'

'But they never will. You know that.' Eve looked over at Luke. 'Really, they always give Jess everything. They just complain about it first.'

'Still not risking it,' Jess insisted.

Eve took her wallet out of her bag and studied the row of cards. 'I haven't used the Bloomie's card in a while.'

She started to pull it free, but Jess grabbed her wrist. 'No, no, no!' Jess exclaimed. 'We're going to go into the city a ton this summer. And what's the city without Bloomingdales?'

'You're right. Hmmm.' Eve studied her cards again. Jess had her wallet out now, and was frowning at her own array.

Luke gave a long, exaggerated sigh. 'Forget it. I think I still have my old library card from Santa Cruz.' He pulled his wallet out of his back pocket. Eve loved how the wallet had worn a white rectangle in the cloth of his jeans.

Luke slid the card between the door jamb and the door, then gave the card a little wiggle. Nothing. He wiggled it a little harder. Eve heard the plastic crack. She and Jess were right to be worried about their cards! One more jiggle. But the door wouldn't budge. 'Maybe you and Jess were right about the card thing,' Luke admitted.

Then the door swung open. Jess stood on the inside grinning at them. 'Unlocked window, round the corner.'

'You shouldn't have gone in by yourself. What if the demon had been waiting for you?' Eve's heart rate increased, thinking about Jess being snatched up by Amunnic.

The smile slid from Jess's face and her eyes went wide. 'You're right.'

*Now I've terrified her*, Eve thought. *Good job.* 'It's OK. We're together now. We need to be careful in there, and not just because Amunnic could be inside,' she said softly. 'This plant isn't on full power, but there's something being produced. I can feel it. And we've all seen what electricity can do.' She flexed her fingers, and she could tell that Luke and Jess were picturing lightning bolts flying out.

Cautiously Eve stepped through the doorway. The large room only had a few fluorescent lights on, their soft electric buzz the only sound. Eve looked around at the large metal tubes with wheels corkscrewing around them – turbines, she remembered from that school field trip – and the catwalk that ran across half the room. The amount of dust on both made the inside of her nose itch, but she didn't catch a whiff of wood-smoke. That was good.

No. Actually it wasn't. They needed Amunnic to be there. They needed to end this before anyone else got sick. They needed to end this while Leo, Briony and Rose were still alive.

*OK, look for demony hiding places*, she instructed herself. She didn't see many places Amunnic could be. Most of the huge space was empty. But there were two rounded, igloo-like things on the other side of the big pipes. They seemed worth checking out.

Eve pointed at them, and Luke and Jess nodded. She started across the cement floor, glad that she was wearing flats so the sound of high heels wouldn't give her away. A shiver ran through her body as she circled around the biggest tube, and she hesitated.

'What?' Jess whispered. 'Do you see something?'

Eve shook her head. She wasn't sure. She just had this feeling . . . She shivered again, and all the fine hairs on her arms and the back of her neck rose. A ferocious static-filled roar suddenly filled her ears, and she gasped.

'Must be one of the turbines,' Luke said loudly.

'You can hear it too?' Eve felt a rush of relief. For a moment she'd thought it was something only she was experiencing, the way she could see the words on the portal when no one else could.

'There's nothing inside those things, and they're the only place to hide. Let's get out of here,' Jess called. 'My ears are about to explode.'

But Eve couldn't move. It felt as if the sound of the turbine was coming from inside her. Her bones shook with it. Even her teeth felt like they were vibrating. Heat flooded her body, the way it did when she was fighting a demon. Her power was churning along with the turbine. Building and building.

She curled her hands into fists. She couldn't let the power out. It was too strong, stronger than it had ever been. If it escaped, she wasn't sure what would happen. She might hurt her friends. But it wanted out. It was pushing at her, fighting her.

Eve squeezed her fists tighter, until her nails dug

into her palms. She screwed her eyes shut, using all her concentration to control the raw energy coursing through her.

It was too much. It was an electric hurricane. An electric tidal wave. So much bigger than she was. Impossible to control or contain. Eve let out a yell. She opened her eyes, opened her fingers. Whatever was going to happen, was going to happen.

Her skin *rippled*. Then sparks began to fly off her. Not just from her fingers, from as much of her body as she could see. In an instant, she was surrounded by a bright whirlwind of them, some white, some red, some yellow, with a few glowing blue and green.

'What's happening?' Jess screamed.

Eve couldn't speak, couldn't attempt to explain. It was exhilarating. She knew it should be terrifying too, but the part of her that would be terrified was slipping away. Her *self* was slipping away.

She was becoming something else, becoming light and heat. Becoming pure energy. Becoming one with—

The turbine cut off abruptly. The lights went out. The room fell into darkness, except for the sparks spinning around Eve. They flared in unison, then went out. Or had they gone *in*? It felt like her body had reabsorbed them. She felt like a live wire, hot and ready.

'Are you . . . are you OK?' Luke reached a hand towards her, then pulled it back quickly, as if he'd been shocked.

'Yeah,' Eve said. 'Actually, I'm great. I'm amazing. I'm . . . God, I can't even describe it!'

'We should leave, in case somebody comes in here trying to get the power back on. I could see inside those igloo-y things. They were empty. Amunnic isn't here. Or Leo and the others.' Jess's voice was calm, but she didn't seem to be able to stop staring at Eve. She led the way to the door, Luke right behind her.

Eve followed, but there was something strange. She felt light on her feet. As if the earth had less gravity, as if she was as close to flying as to walking.

'Look. It's not just the plant that lost power,' Luke said when he stepped outside. 'The whole town's out.'

He was right. Blackness stretched out in front of them as far as the eye could see. Eve blinked, trying to adjust to the darkness. The stars suddenly looked brighter, and almost as if there were more of them than usual. There wasn't a single light on anywhere in Deepdene.

'Did I—? Could I have done that?' Eve asked.

'Why?' Luke's voice was sharp with fear. 'What happened in there?'

'I don't know. I felt like all this energy surged into me.'

'Wow. Really? You think you caused the blackout?' Jess asked.

'There were about a million sparks coming from you,' Luke said slowly. 'I think you might be right. Maybe it's because you were so close to the turbine. All the electricity it was generating was drawn to you.'

They both stared at her, wide-eyed.

'Evie. Are you OK, truly?' Jess asked in a whisper.

'Like I said, I feel awesome. I almost pity Amunnic if we find him tonight,' Eve replied. 'Almost.'

'You'd kick his demon butt in about two seconds,' Jess agreed, eyes still locked on Eve. Eve could tell that she was trying to sound like her normal cheerful self. But there was a current of worry underneath the words.

'It's getting really close to curfew,' Luke said. 'We gotta go.'

'But what about the demon?' Eve asked. 'We didn't find him.'

'My parents were very clear about the curfew,' Jess said nervously. 'They told me it's non-negotiable.'

'We'll have to search for him tomorrow. During daylight. Leo, Briony and Rose are running out of time,' Eve said. She didn't want to go home. She wanted to find Amunnic and kill him. But they had no choice.

After they climbed back over the fence and got a little bit away from the plant, Jess took out her cell-phone to help them see, and Eve added the intense beam of her LED light. As they walked through town, soft candlelight shone through some of the windows.

'Eve and I will walk you home, Jess. I don't think any of us should be alone right now.'

'Fine by me.' Jess was answering Luke, but still looking at Eve.

Luke checked his watch. 'We might be just a couple of minutes late. Not more than that.'

'I won't get in trouble for a couple of minutes. Peter has all the clocks in our house set about fifteen minutes slow,' Jess said. 'That's because he's always late for curfew – his personal one, not the town one – and he decided he could scam our parents.'

'The boy's an evil genius.'

As they walked, Eve noticed that Jess still kept gazing at her. She'd look away for a few seconds, but she always ended up doing it again. 'You do realize you're staring?' Eve said finally. 'You're looking at me like I'm a monster or something.'

'Sorry. But you're wrong. I wasn't thinking you were a monster,' Jess said. 'Back at the plant, with all those sparks flying around you, it was like you'd turned into a goddess or something.'

'Well, don't worry. I'm not planning to make you worship me,' Eve answered.

'That's good. I don't think my dad would approve,' Luke said. 'Thou shalt have no other god but me, and all that.'

'All these houses, and Amunnic could look like any person in any one of them,' Jess commented.

'But he can't change Rose, Briony or Leo's appearance. If – when – we find them, we'll find him too,' Luke reminded her.

They fell silent until they reached Jess's house. 'Just one minute after curfew,' Luke told her.

'You two hurry home,' Jess urged, then turned and ran up to the house. They waited until she slipped inside.

'At least it only takes a few minutes to get home from here. And my parents, thankfully, are over at the clinic again,' Eve said as they started down the street. With every house she passed, she kept thinking about what Jess had said. 'The ability to change appearances, that really does give Amunnic a huge advantage. I mean, you could be him right now, and I wouldn't even know. You could be about to start feeding on my blood.'

'No, you'd know. You'd know because Amunnic would only look like me on the outside. You'd be able to tell the inside wasn't right.' Luke reached out and took her hand. Was he being friendly? More than friendly? Right now, Eve didn't care. Every one of her senses felt like it had been kicked up a notch since she'd taken in all that power, and Luke's skin felt amazing against her own.

'You're right. I'd know.' Eve heard a soft crackling, crunching sound. She tightened her fingers around Luke's. 'Did you hear that?' she whispered.

He shook his head. The sound came again, from somewhere closer. 'Not that time either?'

'Nope.' Luke looked up and down the block. 'I don't see anything, either.'

Eve switched off her light. 'Someone's coming,' she whispered. She pulled Luke over to the weeping willow tree in the Waiteses' front yard, and into the cave created by its low branches. She put her finger to her lips, and waited for the next sound.

*Ker-rack.* Yes, the sounds were definitely getting closer. But Eve's senses were so hyped up. Maybe what she was hearing was a mile away.

Maybe it wasn't, though. Maybe Amunnic had tracked them. Maybe that's what she was hearing.

Her whole body tensed as she heard the sound again. Louder.

*I hope it is him,* she thought. *Jess was right. Tonight, I could kick Amunnic's ass before he even knows what's hit him.* She let go of Luke's hand and tapped her fingers lightly against her thighs, readying herself to snap into action and let some lightning bolts fly.

*Ker-rack.* The sound was almost painfully loud now.

'Cop,' Luke said into her ear. 'Cop eating peanuts, I think,' he added.

Eve turned her head. She could see the police officer pacing the street as clearly as if it was noon instead of nine o'clock at night. 'Cop cop? Or Amunnic cop,' she whispered back. She shifted her weight, and sent one of the tree's long, leafy branches trembling.

The cop jerked his head in their direction. Eve was sure he'd seen her. It had felt like he was looking her straight in the eye. But he didn't approach, he turned and hurried off in the opposite direction.

Eve pulled in a breath, and she swore she could feel each of the little air sacs in her lungs expanding. *How long would her senses stay this way?* she wondered. Then another thought hit her. Would she be able to juice up any time she wanted to? Well, anytime she wanted to and there was a massive turbine around?

It was possible. And who knew what else was possible. Her great-great-great-grandmother had written in her journal that she was still discovering new things she could do with her powers as the Deepdene Witch. So far, Eve had been finding out new things all the time herself. Like the way she'd created that seal over the portal.

Eve and Luke held themselves motionless a few moments more, watching through the branches as the cop, or whatever it had truly been, turned the corner.

They waited a little longer, then left their hiding place. They didn't return to the sidewalk. Instead they cut across lawns and gardens, keeping to the shadows, until they reached Eve's house. The phone was ringing as they went inside. Eve hurried to the kitchen and grabbed it.

'Just wanted to make sure you're home. I didn't

think you'd forget about the new curfew, but I wanted to be sure,' her mother said.

'Nope, didn't forget.' *Didn't keep curfew*, she thought, *but definitely didn't forget.*

'The clinic has a back-up generator, which we just got working, but I guess you and Luke are stuck in the dark,' her mom continued.

'Yeah, but we're OK. We have lots of candles.' In fact, Luke had already found some and was lighting them.

'I guess you'll have to eat something cold. Try to get in something nutritious before you hit the ice cream before it melts, OK?'

'We will, Mom. See you when you get home.' Eve said goodbye, then hung up. 'You hungry?' she asked Luke.

'Demon-hunting and cop – or whatever – evading always gives me an appetite,' he answered.

Eve opened the freezer. 'Ice cream?' she suggested.

Luke looked over her shoulder. 'Is that lasagne? I love lasagne.'

'That is one frozen solid block of lasagne. I could get you an ice pick if you want. Or . . .' Eve smiled. She really didn't know everything she could do with her power, especially when she was juiced. She took the lasagne out of the freezer and pulled off the cling film covering it.

'The ice cream's probably a better idea,' Luke said. 'Even thawing it would take for ever.'

'For ever for somebody who isn't the Deepdene Witch.' Eve aimed her fingers at the lasagne and let her power fly. The cheese on top instantly melted and a whoosh of steam erupted from the pasta. 'Bing!' she cried, triumphant. What a cool way to be able to use her zappy fingers.

Luke blinked. 'You rock so hard,' he said.

Eve's smile widened into a grin. 'It's good to have a friend with superpowers, isn't it?' She had superpowers! She'd never thought about it exactly that way before. She took a couple of plates from the cabinet, then served up the lasagne. It didn't hit her until they both sat down at the table how totally romantic the meal would be. Just the two of them. In the candlelight.

Totally distracting.

But for now, she didn't care. Tonight, she was just going to enjoy it.

*Man*, Luke thought. *I just keep getting thrown into these über-romantic situations with Eve. First not-quite-double-dating with Jess and Seth, and now eating dinner alone together in the candlelight.* Not that he was complaining. It did make things confusing, though. They were always ending up in boyfriend–girlfriend type situations, but they were just friends. He was up for more. But was she?

Now was not the time to try to find out. Not until the town was safe – his dad, Seth, Leo, Briony, Rose, and everybody. He took a bite of lasagne, then realized that Eve was staring at him.

'Do I have sauce on my face?' he asked.

Eve shook her head.

'Are you still worried about me being Amunnic?' Luke asked. 'Amunnic drinks blood. He doesn't eat lasagne. Hence, I am not he.'

Eve laughed. 'I wasn't worried. I was just thinking it's cool that I know the inner you so well.'

'I think it's cool too. Not that you know me that well,' he added quickly. 'Although I guess that actually is cool. But that I've gotten to know you too.'

'And find out that I occasionally think about something other than bags and shoes?' Eve said.

'A lot more than occasionally.' The more he got to know the inner Eve, the more bowled over he was by her. And he'd been bowled over by the outer Eve since day one. Tonight she looked more beautiful than ever, with the candlelight bathing her face in a golden glow, and glinting off her shiny dark curls.

He had to kiss her. Had to. Right now. It would be physically impossible to resist. He reached out to move the candles out of the way . . . and the phone rang. Eve started, knocking her glass of iced tea to the floor. She winced as the glass shattered, then gestured for him to get the phone while she knelt down to pick up the pieces.

Luke grabbed the phone off the wall cradle. 'Hello? Evergold residence.' He had grown up answering the phone in a sort of formal way, since you never knew who might be calling the rectory.

'Hey, it's me. At the Meredith residence,' Jess said. 'I just wanted to figure out when we should meet up tomorrow.'

'Early,' Luke said. 'We have to figure out more places to search for Amunnic.'

'So right after breakfast?' Jess asked.

'Sounds good,' Luke replied. He turned to Eve. 'Setting up when to meet Jess in the a.m.' Eve nodded as she brushed slivers of glass into a dustpan.

'So what are you two up to?' Jess asked.

'Just eating dinner. Eve figured out this amazing

new thing she can do with her zap. She used it to basically nuke a frozen lasagne,' Luke told her.

'Hmmm. Just the two of you. Eating dinner. And I'm guessing by candlelight,' Jess said.

'It's harder to find your mouth with the fork in the dark,' Luke joked.

'Sounds very romantic.' Jess sighed. 'And I'm left out of the fun. Not that it would continue to be romantic if I were there.'

Luke glanced over at Eve. He'd been thinking how romantic the situation had been. Jess obviously thought it was too. But had Eve felt the big R?

'Peter is trying to see how much ice cream he can fit in his head before it melts. The ice cream, not the head,' Jess continued. 'I'm hoping the piglet gets the massive case of brain freeze he deserves.'

In the background Luke heard a muffled 'Hey!'

'If I want any dessert, I have to go fight for it,' Jess said. 'Ooh, the lights just came back on! Did they over there?'

'Yep. Right this second,' Luke said.

'Well, turn them off again so you can still use the candles,' Jess suggested. 'Come by my house in the morning, OK? Being out alone, even in the day-time, it's . . . you know.'

'We'll pick you up, no problem,' Luke told her. 'See you soon. Bye.'

Luke hung up the phone. 'Jess said Peter's eating all the ice cream,' he said. Lame. But somehow, with the lights back on, he felt awkward and wasn't sure what to say. The lame words had just come out on their own.

'Sounds like him,' Eve said. She sat back down at the table and blew out the candles. So she wasn't interested in trying to get the romantic mood back.

'I think I'm gonna take this up to my room.' Luke picked up his plate of lasagne. 'I want to check my email and I'll maybe try and tackle those books I brought from the church.'

'OK. I'll just . . . watch TV, I guess.' Eve picked up the remote.

Luke hesitated for a second, then left the kitchen and went to his room. *I can't believe I'm all worried about Eve and romance and whether or not she wants me to kiss her*, he thought. *We didn't find Amunnic tonight. That means my dad is still being eaten up by the plague, along with so many others.*

The harsh thoughts pounded at him. And maybe tonight the demon would snatch another victim. An image of the whole town, dead, filled his mind.

Some taken by the plague, some drained of blood.

'Nothing you can do about it right now,' he muttered aloud. *Tomorrow*, he promised himself. *Tomorrow we'll track down Amunnic and kill him.*

But could three teenagers really save the town? Even if one of them was the Deepdene Witch?

# Chapter Six

Eve took a last look in the bathroom mirror. She'd pulled her long, dark hair into a loose knot on top of her head, with a few tendrils falling down to frame her face, and she'd gone light with her make-up, just some pale lip gloss, mascara, and a little powder to keep her face from getting too shiny in the hot sun.

There was no reason not to look as pretty as possible when going after a demon. *Especially when Luke is part of the demon-fighting team*, a little voice inside her head whispered.

'Not the time to get distracted by boys,' she told her reflection, looking herself sternly in the eye. Huh. Her eyes looked bluer than usual today. Sparklier. She felt sparkly too. Like all that energy she'd sucked up at the power plant was still coursing through her.

She looked at the row of round light bulbs along the top of the mirror, imaging the current feeding them. Could she absorb it too? Her fingers started to tingle, and she itched to experiment, but it would have to wait. She was about to be late for breakfast.

She turned and headed downstairs to the kitchen. Her parents were already at the kitchen table, watching the news on TV and eating breakfast. Eve decided to pass on the bagels, yogurt and fruit. She prepared herself for a lecture as she took the box of Count Chocula from the cereal shelf of the cupboard. Her mother just didn't comprehend how sometimes a girl needed something chocolate for breakfast. One of those times was when demon encounter was likely to occur soon.

'Eve, that's barely acceptable as a snack. It's certainly not—' her mother began.

Eve flipped over the box, and began the argument she always used. 'It has thirty per cent of the daily requirement of riboflavin, iron and—'

Luke came through the side door, letting it slam shut behind him. He was so completely yummy, especially right now in his jogging shorts and sleeveless T, a sheen of sweat glossing his arms and shoulders, and his hair all tousled.

Eve used the interruption to fill her bowl and sit down at the table. Her mother shook her head at her. 'Luke, breakfast with the Count?' Eve asked.

'I think I'll stick with a bagel.' He sat down and took one from the plate. 'Good morning, all,' he added to her parents. They both really liked him. He seemed to like them too. Eve found it both great and a little bit annoying that he'd become so comfortable in her home so fast.

'What's it like out there?' Eve's father asked Luke.

'I ran past the church. It has a huge tent over it and guards posted out front. I asked what was going on, and they said the CDC was starting to fumigate the buildings where large numbers of people gathered. They'll be working their way through the town,' he answered.

'That's a start,' Eve's mother said.

'They also told me my dad had been moved over to the courthouse. They want all the plague victims there. It's too hard for the aid workers to go from house to house now that there are so many people sick.'

'We've started sending people directly from the clinic to the courthouse,' Eve's mom told him. 'There are a lot of great medical workers taking care of them, Luke. Your dad might have a private room in a hospital if things were different, but I promise you he wouldn't get more knowledgeable doctors or better treatment.'

'I still can't believe how fast they got the town closed off,' Luke commented. He clearly wasn't up to having a conversation about his father.

'It needed to happen,' Eve's dad said. 'They have to keep Flu X contained.' He grimaced. 'But when I see those spirals of barbed wire on top of the fence, I feel like we've all been sentenced to prison.'

'They're talking about Deepdene.' Eve's mother upped the volume on the news.

'A new story from Deepdene, New York, this morning,' the newscaster announced. 'Another citizen from the town is reportedly missing – nineteen-year-old Cathy Jenkins.'

'Cathy. That's Leo Mackenzie's girlfriend!' Eve exclaimed, just as the words 'High School Sweethearts in Escape Pact?' appeared on the screen above Cathy and Leo's senior prom picture.

'I don't like the sound of this,' Eve's dad said, twisting round in his chair to get a better view of the TV. They all listened in silence as the newscaster explained that Cathy's parents had reported her missing when she hadn't returned home by curfew the night before. They were afraid she'd gotten ill and fainted and needed help, but a search of the town hadn't come up with any trace of her. The police were speculating that Cathy had sneaked out of town, possibly on one of the trucks that had been allowed in and out of Deepdene bringing supplies, to meet up with Leo.

'The contagion spreads so fast.' Eve's mom shook her head. 'I hate to even think about Leo and Cathy on the outside. They could be passing the virus on even if they haven't contracted the flu. It's not just them, either. A number of people who had been exposed left town before the lockdown.'

*And some people that everyone assumes got out probably didn't,* Eve thought. She guessed it was possible that Rose and Briony had run away from town without saying anything to their parents or friends. She really, really hoped that was what happened. But she couldn't make herself believe it was.

'Let's hope they didn't get far if they are out there,' Eve's dad added. 'The last thing we need is for this disease to spread to another town. Or, God forbid, into the city.'

Luke and Eve exchanged a glance. Eve knew he was thinking the same thing she was: the demon had captured Cathy too.

'Do you think it's possible, you know, that Cathy

got out on a truck?' Eve asked. 'Would they even let a truck past the guard house?'

'Medical supplies are still being brought in,' her mom answered. 'And there are plans in the works to bring in food. So just a few authorized trucks will be going in and out.'

'I'm sure they'll be searched,' her dad added. 'But I suppose it's possible Cathy could have hidden herself well enough to get through.'

*Possible, but not likely*, Eve thought. The likely scenario was that Amunnic was feeding on the blood of Cathy and the other quote-unquote missing people right that second.

'I'm still not sure we should be doing research right now,' Jess said as she, Eve and Luke walked towards the library a little more than an hour later. Every house that had had a plague victim was cordoned off with yellow police tape. Since no one knew how the plague spread, those houses weren't considered safe for healthy people.

'Like we were saying yesterday, Deepdene isn't that big. Shouldn't we just keep searching for Amunnic's hiding place?' Jess asked.

'I just started thinking this might be faster,' Luke

answered. 'I started picturing the empty summer places – any of them could be where the demon has Briony and the others. Some research might help us figure out the best places to look.'

'The Deepdene library has a big occult section – I guess having a portal to hell will do that to a town,' Eve added. 'A lot of the books are really old. We might get lucky and find something that wasn't online. Something that can narrow down the search and help us find Amunnic faster. Like that he prefers a view of the sunrise from his bedroom window,' she joked weakly.

Jess shot her a sharp look. 'Not funny,' she said.

'Sorry,' Eve said. 'Stress-induced bad joke.' But she didn't feel stressed. Her body felt light, as if gravity wasn't having its usual pull. Walking seemed to take almost no effort at all. *Must be all that voltage I absorbed*, she decided.

Eve caught sight of Megan coming round the corner. Megan's Dalmatian, Freckles, spotted them a second later, and started barking wildly and rearing up on his back legs like he thought he was a horse.

'We see you. We're coming to say hi,' Jess called to the excited dog.

'I hope you're coming to say hi to me too,' Megan joked when they reached her.

'Well, Freckles first, or he might explode,' Eve said. She and Jess both knelt down and patted the dog until he became as close to calm as he was able to get. Luke contributed by scratching him behind both ears.

'Hi, Megan,' Jess said as she straightened up.

'Hi, Megan,' Eve and Luke echoed.

Megan laughed, but only for a second. Then her expression became serious. 'I had to get out of the house,' she said. 'My mom keeps staring at me, looking for any signs that I've got it. Which I understand, but it's driving me insane. Joss Elroy has it now. And Mr Neemy. Mollie too. It was so weird to be on Main yesterday and not smell cookies baking.'

Eve shook her head sadly. It was just wrong to think of a Thursday without Mollie's Market filling the street with the smell of chocolate, cinnamon, peanut butter and general yumminess. Pieces of Deepdene were being stripped away every day the plague continued.

'Have you seen the craziness on Facebook?' Megan asked.

'No. What's up?' With everything that had been going on, Eve hadn't checked any of her usual sites for a couple of days.

'There are all these theories flying around about what's happening in Deepdene,' Megan said.

'What kind of theories?' Luke asked, and Eve knew he was thinking about the demon.

'A bunch of people are blaming aliens, if you can believe that,' Megan explained. 'They're saying the aliens designed the plague to wipe out humans so Earth can be colonized. Then there are people who think the government is testing some kind of chemical weapon on the town. A few people are saying Flu X virus is actually intelligent. That it has consciousness and is doing this to us on purpose.'

'I guess you heard the news about Cathy Jenkins,' Jess said.

'Yeah. I've been trying to call her. Same deal as Leo. I keep getting sent straight to voicemail,' Megan said. 'I'm sure they're together. Cathy wouldn't have been able to deal with Leo on one side of the fence and her on the other. They've been going out since seventh grade,' she added to Luke.

'We should probably get going,' Eve said, her mind suddenly filled with the image of Leo and Cathy drained of blood.

'Going where?' Megan asked. 'I want to come.'

'The library,' Jess told her.

Megan scrunched up her nose. 'Really? Like for homework? We don't even know when school's going to open again.'

'It's just something to do,' Luke said. He gave Freckles another double ear scratch. 'Sorry, bud. No dogs allowed.'

'My mom will probably panic if I don't come home soon anyway,' Megan said. 'I'll see you guys.'

Eve picked up her pace. She was praying that Luke was right and that one of the books in the library would give them something they could use to track the demon.

'It's open! I wasn't sure it would be,' Jess exclaimed when they reached the library's wide front steps.

They didn't need to use one of the library computers to find shelf numbers. They already knew where the books on demons were kept. Eve, Jess and Luke each grabbed an armful and sat down at the nearest table.

Eve found Amunnic in the index of the third book she opened. There was just a short entry. 'It says here that a merchant ship ran aground in Ephesus with all the crew drained of blood. They burned the ship and prayed for deliverance from the demon Amunnic.' She put the book aside. 'Ephesus is in Turkey, I think. That must have been before the demon got to Egypt.'

'Not helpful.' Jess looked pale, her eyes rimmed with red. She'd probably gotten hardly any sleep the past couple of nights. Eve was pretty sure she wouldn't be able to sleep if Luke was lying in one of those beds in the courthouse with his skin rotting away. Not that Luke was her boyfriend the way Seth was Jess's.

Eve chose another book and checked the index. There was no Amunnic listed. Nothing under 'Many Faces' either. She started to put the book in the 'done' pile, then realized she ought to search by traits too. There were a bunch of pages listed for 'blood drinkers'. Most were about vampires, although one page had a brief mention of hellhounds feeding on blood, and there were a couple of pages about the chupacabra, a creature with spines all down its back that supposedly fed mainly on goat blood.

'Ugh. Did you know some Russian nomads used to drink the blood of the first enemy they killed in battle?' Jess asked. She'd clearly been searching for blood drinkers too.

They all fell silent as they continued to search for anything that could refer to Amunnic. The words had started looking like streams of black ink to Eve, when Luke spoke up.

'I think I found something good,' he announced. 'Or not good, but important. It's about how Amunnic kills people.'

'Don't we know that already?' Jess asked. 'He drains their blood. That pretty much kills anyone.'

'He does drink human blood according to this, but there's a whole ritual involved,' Luke explained. 'First Amunnic uses one claw to—'

'Claw? I hate it when they have claws,' Eve interrupted. 'Sorry, go on.'

'The demon uses a claw to open one of its victim's veins,' Luke continued. 'The blood floods out, and Amunnic catches it in a ceremonial ceramic bowl. He has to say an incantation over the blood, and then drink it while it is still warm. The book also says that Amunnic keeps his victims alive for several weeks, taking blood whenever he thirsts.'

Jess swallowed hard enough for Eve to hear. 'So this demon basically uses people as living wine bottles. Just keeps them around, and drinks when he feels like it.'

'Yeah.' Luke rubbed the back of his neck. 'Yeah,' he said again.

'Keeping his victims alive could be a good thing,' Eve said. 'I mean, it's hideous. But it means that everyone Amunnic has taken is probably still alive.' She reached across the table and pulled the book Luke had been reading over in front of her. 'The bowl even says Amunnic on it,' she commented. 'How old must that thing be?'

She looked up and found Luke and Jess staring at her. 'Where are you getting that?' Luke asked. 'The name?'

Eve tapped the markings around the top of the bowl in the drawing. 'Right there.'

Neither Luke or Jess said a word. 'Oh,' Eve said, getting it. 'What do you see around the top?'

'Just a bunch of geometric shapes,' Luke answered, and Jess nodded along with him. 'But you see something else, don't you?'

'Letters,' Eve replied. 'A.M.U.N.N.I.C.' She sank back down onto her chair, a little shaken. 'I guess it's a Deepdene Witch thing, huh?'

'Well, this is the second time it's happened,' Luke said gently. 'You could read what was written on the arch leading to the portal, even though Jess and I couldn't.'

'Part of your demon-fighting arsenal,' Jess said.

Eve started to shove the book back to Luke, but a paragraph near the bottom of the page caught her eye. *This could be what we need*, she thought.

'What? Do you see something else on the bowl?' Luke leaned close.

'No. But it's about why Amunnic hasn't been sighted since approximately 600 BC,' she told him. 'Legend has it that around that time Many Faces was weak from hunger. He was so weak, in fact, that an Arabian magician was able to trap him inside a ceramic vessel.' Eve tapped the drawing of the bowl. 'This. The same bowl he used to drink blood.'

'It seems like Mr Dokey brought back a really cool souvenir from Egypt,' Luke said. 'We've got to go talk to him. We have to find out whether he has that bowl.'

'Amunnic's clearly not in it any more,' Jess said. She sounded exhausted.

'But he needs the bowl to feed,' Eve reminded her. 'Which is pretty much the same as needing the bowl to survive. We find the bowl, we find the demon.' She stood up. 'Field trip to the plague ward, anyone?'

'You know what I just realized,' Jess said on their way to the courthouse. 'Everyone the demon has taken is around our age.'

'Maybe younger blood is more powerful. Like more vitamins per serving,' Eve suggested.

'Then why wouldn't he be taking kids?' Luke asked.

A slash of revulsion cut through Eve as she considered his question. 'Maybe it likes all the extra hormones,' she suggested. 'My mom is always telling me how teenagers are raging with them.'

'It could actually be something like that,' Luke commented. 'I know you were half kidding, but animals are really sensitive to the scent of hormones. Maybe a demon could be too.'

'None of the people taken were sick, at least that we know of,' Jess said. 'I mean, none of them was showing symptoms, right?'

'You're right!' Eve exclaimed. 'So maybe Amunnic can't feed on people with the plague.'

'The curse makes more sense then.' Luke slowed down a little as he explained his theory. 'It doesn't just warn people that the demon is nearby, it makes it a lot harder for Amunnic to feed, which could make him weaker.'

'Maybe weak enough so that magician could trap him,' Jess offered. 'The priest's curse was better than I was giving it credit for. If we're right, and Amunnic can't feed on plague victims, maybe that led to him getting weak enough to be captured.'

'Look at these guys,' Eve said, jerking her chin at Dave and a couple of his buddies – Phillip and Sean – heading towards them, all wearing bathing suits and flip-flops and carrying rolled-up towels. Dave and Phillip each had a grip on one of the handles of a big cooler.

'Party down at the beach,' Sean announced.

Phillip released his side of the cooler and it slammed to the sidewalk a couple of metres away from Eve.

'Dude!' Dave exclaimed, still gripping the other handle. 'What the hell?'

Phillip stared at him, blinking. 'Slipped.' He clenched and unclenched his hand.

Eve suspected it was less that his hand had slipped than that Phillip was feeling weak. He was sort of swaying on his feet, like he was on a sailboat.

Jess moved closer to Eve. 'I think he might have it,' she whispered. Eve nodded, taking a step back, as if that would protect her.

'You guys want to come?' Sean asked. He winked at Jess and Eve. 'We could use some lovely ladies.' *He doesn't look that great either*, Eve realized. Under his tan, his skin had an ashen tone, and his hair was damp with sweat. 'You won't be the only ones,' he added. 'Megan and Elisha are meeting us.'

'We severely need some beach time. We just want to hang and not think about anything,' Dave added. And they all knew exactly what he meant by 'anything'.

'Maybe later,' Jess told them. 'I promised my mom I'd be home by one, and she'll have a meltdown if I don't show. Have fun, guys.' She circled around them, Eve and Luke right behind her. Eve held her breath as she went by, hoping that would protect her, although it felt like the crackling current still whisking through her would annihilate any virus that dared to invade her body.

'Pretty soon the healthy people will be living in the courthouse,' Luke said. 'There will be a lot fewer of them than plague victims.'

'Not going to happen. Pretty soon Amunnic will be gone,' Eve vowed. 'I'm zapping him right back to hell.'

'I like your style,' Luke told her as they climbed the courthouse steps. A guard in a hazmat suit was positioned in front of the big double doors.

'No one allowed in,' the guard told them.

'We're here to visit my boyfriend, Seth Schneider,' Jess said firmly. 'It's OK if we wear hazmat suits. I did it the other day.'

The guard gestured for them to stay where they were, and opened the door. 'This girl says she was allowed to visit a victim,' he called to a nurse doing paperwork at a long table that had been set up in the lobby.

Jess moved closer so the nurse could see her. The nurse nodded. 'She was given approval. She has to get into a suit though.'

The guard stepped back to allow them inside. 'Wait. The other two don't have authorization,' the nurse said when she saw Luke and Eve following Jess.

'But they're with me,' Jess protested.

'Don't press it, miss,' the nurse told her. 'You're lucky to get in yourself. The only reason you're allowed is because my supervisor has a weakness for tears. I don't.'

'Neither do I,' the guard said.

'Fine.' Jess turned to Eve and Luke. 'I'll tell *him* you said hi.'

Eve and Luke reluctantly turned round and stepped back outside. 'I want to hear what Dokey has to say,' Luke said as they walked down the steps.

'Me too. There's got to be another way in,' Eve answered. They circled around the building. 'Fire door,' she pointed out.

'The alarm will go off it we try to get in that way though,' Luke said. Eve nodded and kept walking, then she stopped. 'What?' Luke asked.

'What if I zap it?' Eve stared at the door's DO NOT ENTER sign.

'The door? How would that—'

'Not the door. The alarm. You open the door, and I zap the alarm before it can go off,' Eve explained.

Luke raised his eyes brows. 'It might work. A power surge could short it out.'

'Let's try.' Eve did a guard check. There wasn't one in sight. She and Luke hurried over to the door.

'On three,' Luke said. 'One ... two ... three!' He shoved the door open. Eve darted through, spotted the alarm box, and thrust her hands towards it. She hit it with so much power that it melted before it could give a peep.

'Nice,' Luke told her.

The hallway was empty. They started opening doors, just a crack, looking for suits.

'There are a bunch in here in a big cart. Looks like they've already been worn and need to be sterilized,' Luke said as he peered into the third room on the right.

'Good enough,' Eve said. 'Face it. It's not like we

both haven't been exposed to the plague multiple times already.'

They ducked inside and suited up. No one would question them now, Eve thought. They looked as official as anyone once their clothes were covered and the masks were obscuring their faces.

'Let's find Mr Dokey,' Luke said as they returned to the hallway.

'And Jess,' Eve added. She strode over to the next room and cracked the door. 'Score!' She waved Luke over and led the way inside. A computer sat on the desk of the small clerk's office. 'Bet they're using it to track patients and treatments,' she said.

Luke was at the keyboard before the last word was out of her mouth. 'Dokey's in room two-o-seven. They have him listed as patient zero. That means he was the first one with the plague.'

'Get Seth's room too,' Eve said.

Luke typed in *Schneider, Seth*. 'In courtroom A, bed sixteen.'

Eve had to stifle a gasp when they found the court-room and stepped inside. Cots lined the walls and aisles between the wooden benches. So many people, all so sick. Eve was thankful for the thick plastic of her visor. It made everything seem a little distant, a little less real.

She didn't need to use the bed number to find Seth. Eve quickly spotted Jess standing over him. Her shoulders were heaving with sobs. 'This way,' she said to Luke, then rushed over to join her friend.

'He doesn't even know I'm here. I can't even tell him I'm sorry I ran off the other day,' Jess cried when Eve put her arm round Jess's shoulders. Seth's eyes were open, but glazed. She didn't think he was seeing anything. Was he even conscious? Jess seemed pretty out of it too, not even stopping to question how Luke and Eve had made it into the courthouse. Eve knew that seeing Seth in that state was more than her bestie could handle.

'He knows you're with him,' Luke told her. 'People always know, even if they can't show it. He knows and it's helping him.'

Luke was so good at giving comfort, Eve thought. Maybe it was because his dad was a minister and Luke had spent a lot of time going out on calls with him. 'We need to get to Mr Dokey,' Eve said gently.

'I don't want to leave him.' Jess rested her gloved hand lightly on Seth's chest. His lips parted slightly, as if he was about to speak, but he didn't utter a sound.

'The best thing you can do for him is help us find Amunnic,' Luke reminded her.

Jess sucked in a deep breath. 'OK, yes, you're right.' She blinked rapidly to clear her eyes of tears. There was no way to wipe them through the mask of the hazmat suit.

'He's in room two-o-seven,' Eve said. She linked her arm through Jess's and guided her out of the ward and over to the stairs.

Luke held up one hand when they reached the first floor. He backed down a few steps, Eve and Jess following his lead. 'Guard in front of the door I think is Dokey's,' he said softly.

'I got it,' Jess said.

Eve didn't have a chance to ask what she meant. Jess threw herself up the stairs, screaming. 'Seth! He's dying! Somebody has to do something.' Eve could tell the hysteria in her friend's voice wasn't completely put on.

Luke and Eve crept back to the top of the stairs. Jess had the guard facing away from them and had managed to pull him several steps away from the door. *Now or never*, Eve thought. She darted towards the door and slipped behind. Luke shut the door as soon as he followed her inside.

'Oh my God,' Eve whispered. 'Is that him?' The figure on the cot that had been placed to one side of the desk in the judge's chambers didn't look like Mr Dokey. It didn't even look human.

Cautiously Eve moved forward. Now she was able to make out a nose almost eaten away by the necrosis and lips that were raw and oozing. The mouth was open, revealing a thick puffy tongue, bright angry red, except for where splotches of rot like damp black fungus had sprouted. The eyes were shut. Eve was grateful for that. She didn't want to see what the plague had done to the eyes.

'Mr Dokey?' She was still having trouble believing it was her teacher. 'Mr Dokey?' she said more loudly. No response.

Eve reached out and laid her hand on Mr Dokey's. Through the glove, she felt the skin on his hand slide. Bile splashed up in her throat when she raised her gloved fingers to her eyes and saw the greenish-black smear. A piece of Mr Dokey's skin had peeled away at Eve's gentle touch.

# Chapter Seven

Eve's eyes jerked back to Mr Dokey's hand, and she caught a glimpse of white bone where his skin had peeled away. She heard a low whimpering sound and it took her a moment to realize it was coming from her own throat.

Luke stepped up beside her and grabbed her hand. Even through two layers of gloves she could feel its warmth, and it helped steady her. 'Mr Dokey!' she exclaimed. 'It's Luke Thompson and Eve Evergold.'

'From school. Can you hear us?' Luke added.

Mr Dokey's eyelids fluttered. When they opened, oily-looking black strands connected the upper and lower lids.

'Hi. Hi, Mr Dokey. It's good to see you,' Eve said, forcing herself to treat him as the person he was, even though he looked like a monster. She wondered if he could see her or anything at all.

Jess slipped up beside her and Luke. 'I got rid of the guard, at least for a little,' she said. Her body stiffened as she took in Mr Dokey's appearance. 'Is that going to happen to everyone?' she asked softly. 'I can't even— Can you even see a patch of skin that isn't . . . that isn't covered?'

Eve shook her head. 'We have to stay focused.'

'We wanted to find out about the bowl,' Luke said loudly. 'You brought a bowl back from Egypt, didn't you, Mr Dokey?'

Mr Dokey's frail body spasmed, and he muttered some words that Eve couldn't make out. She wasn't even sure they were in English.

'The bowl. The ceramic bowl. Where is it?' Jess urged.

Mr Dokey gave another spasm, one so hard it lifted his spine off the bed. 'I did this. Me.' His voice was thick and muffled. He twisted his head back and forth, and Eve saw pieces of skin appear on his pillowcase.

'Calm down, please,' she begged. 'You're hurting yourself.'

'Warned!' Mr Dokey cried out. 'Warned. Didn't— Wouldn't. My fault.'

'It's OK,' Luke told him. 'It's going to be OK,

Mr Dokey. We just need to know where that bowl is.'

'We can save everybody!' Jess added.

'She's right,' Luke said, enunciating each word clearly. 'We can stop this. All of this.'

Mr Dokey blinked, frowning. His eyes seemed to lock on Luke's face. They were full of pleading. 'You know where,' he rasped. 'You know.' Then his eyes shut again, and his body went limp. It was as if he'd used all the strength he had.

'He didn't— He's not dead, is he?' Jess asked.

Luke shook his head. 'I think he just exhausted himself. We're not going to get any more out of him. But it seemed like we were right. He knew what we were talking about when we brought up the bowl. It's here in Deepdene.'

'Yeah,' Eve agreed. 'And he said *you* knew where.'


'I hate this!' Jess burst out as soon as they left the courthouse. 'I just hate it. I want something to punch. I'm so mad about everything. About Seth getting sick, and your dad, Luke. And about there being another stupid demon in our town.'

'When we find stupid Amunnic you can punch him,' Eve told her. 'I'll use my zaps to hold him still for you.'

Jess shook out her arms. Eve could tell she was trying to let go of some of the tension in her body. 'So what do you think Mr Dokey was talking about? Why would you know where the bowl is?' she asked Luke.

'All I can think of is the church,' Luke answered. 'That's the only place that I'd know that you two might not, right?'

'I don't know if he even realized what he was saying,' Eve replied. 'All that stuff he was saying about a warning – what was that supposed to mean?'

'The demon couldn't go in the church, could it?' Jess asked. 'Not with the gargoyles.'

The Deepdene church was filled with gargoyles, hundreds of them, all sizes and types. They'd discovered the stone monsters had been placed there to keep the church safe from demons.

'Right. The gargoyles,' Luke said. 'Maybe under the church? That's where I hid the sword. There's a crypt down there, but no gargoyles.'

'We should check it out,' Eve answered. 'I don't know why Mr Dokey would think it was down there though. He wouldn't have taken it there.'

'I want to get the sword anyway,' Luke said. 'It might not feel like it, but we're getting closer to Amunnic. I'd feel better having it with us. I think we're going to have to wait until after curfew though.'

'Why? Just for the extra challenge?' Jess demanded. She ran her fingers through her hair. Wearing the hazmat mask had made it damp and limp.

'They're fumigating the church. There are a bunch of CDC personnel over there. No way can we just walk in,' Luke told her. 'I don't think they'll keep working after curfew.'

'What do we do until then?' Eve asked.

'I really do need to hit something,' Jess said. 'Master Justin has a class later. I'm going. Maybe he'll let me try to chop a board in half or something.'

'I'll go with you,' Eve told Jess. Her bestie needed her – that was clear. Seeing Seth, and seeing what the plague had done to Mr Dokey, had devastated Jess. Eve looked over at Luke. 'I think you're right about getting the sword before we go further. Right after curfew we'll get it and check out the church.'

*We have to find Amunnic tonight,* she thought. *Mr Dokey can't last much longer, and soon the others will be in as horrible a condition as he is.*

'Three more minutes,' Master Justin said.

Eve shot a glance at Jess. They were the only two

162

students in the kung-fu class. Jess's legs were trembling, and sweat had pasted her hair to her head. Eve was feeling like she could hold the horse stance all night, where you basically held your body in the position it would be in if you were riding a horse – only without the horse.

*I bet I could hold it all day tomorrow too*, Eve thought, *if I just took a little sip of the current that's powering the studio's lights.* It was like she had an almost endless power source available to her. She just had to learn how to take the power a little at a time. She couldn't go around causing blackouts the way she had last night.

Jess let out a little groan. *This has to be really hard*, Eve thought. Jess was such an athlete. She always got assigned the hardest gymnastic moves in her cheer-leading routines. Maybe all the worry about Seth was sucking the strength and energy out of her.

'All right, very good,' Master Justin finally told Eve and Jess. 'Now, stay in that position and we'll do some side kicks.'

*Just imagine there's a demon over there, and you're kicking it right in the belly*, Eve coached herself. She felt electric jolts through her leg with every kick. It felt awesome.

'That was a lot more fun than I thought it would be,' Eve told Jess as they left the dojo above the hardware store.

'You know what would be more fun? If you carried me down these stairs,' Jess answered.

'Tiring, huh? But did it make you feel any better?' Eve asked.

Jess scrubbed her face with her fingers. 'The best I can say is that it exhausted me to the point where I don't think I have the energy to feel anything at all.'

'If you really want me to give you a piggy-back ride, I will,' Eve said.

Jess shook her head. 'If I get on, I might not be able to get back off.' She grabbed the stair rail with one hand as they slowly walked down the stairs together.

As they stepped outside, Eve could feel stored heat being released from the cement sidewalk. If possible, today was even hotter than yesterday. 'You know what I wish?' she asked as she looked longingly down at Big Ola's – which was now closed, along with every other place on Main Street. 'I wish I could bathe in ice cream. How deliciously wonderful would that feel, to be immersed in sweet, sweet coldness?'

The idea seemed to revive Jess a tiny bit. 'Cleopatra used to take baths in milk,' she said. She knew pretty much every beauty factoid in existence. 'That makes me think it's great for the skin. So I'm in on the ice-cream-bathing plan.'

'If this heat wave keeps going, we'll buy up every bit of ice cream we can find and fill up the pool,' Eve promised her. She glanced at her watch. 'Not even an hour and a half until it's time to search the church. We'll have just enough time to shower and change.'

'Maybe my stench would be good demon repellent,' Jess joked, but her voice didn't hold its usual lightness.

A long, shrill wail drowned out the sound of Eve's laugh. 'What was that?' she exclaimed, already running towards the sound. She whipped round the corner just in time to see Sean collapse to his knees on the sidewalk.

*Plague*, Eve thought. She remembered that he had looked really pale earlier.

'He took them! Both of them!' Sean howled as Eve skidded to a stop next to him.

'Who? Who took who?' Jess exclaimed, panting with the exertion of running after Eve.

'Phillip. He took them. We were on the beach, and he grabbed them. Dave and Elisha. Megan went home before that,' Sean explained. Eve could see him struggling to get a grip on himself, but it wasn't working.

'Phillip took them? Where?' Jess asked, kneeling next to Sean.

'I don't know. It was like Phillip had a complete personality change. He started growling, actually growling. Then he was clawing people.'

'Clawing?' Eve repeated.

'I know. It sounds crazy, but it's true,' Sean swore.

'I'm calling an ambulance for you,' Jess told Sean, pulling out her cell.

'It doesn't sound crazy. We believe you,' Eve reassured him. She knew exactly what had happened. It hadn't been Phillip they'd seen with the other guys that morning. It had been the demon. That's why Phillip had seemed so out of it and awkward, not because he was getting sick.

Amunnic had been standing right in front of Eve only hours before. Amunnic wearing Phillip's face.

# Chapter Eight

Eve and Jess watched in silence as the ambulance carrying Sean disappeared from sight, blue light spinning.

'This proves we were right about Amunnic only feeding on healthy people,' Eve said. 'That's why he didn't take Sean.'

'I guess there is a reason I should be glad Seth has it.' Jess's voice was flat and lifeless.

'Yeah. See, always a silver lining.' Eve gave a grim smile. 'Let's go tell Luke Amunnic has Dave and Elisha now too.' She wrapped one arm round Jess's shoulders. Jess leaned heavily against her as they started back to Eve's.

'This is all going to be over soon. I promise,' Eve told Jess, hoping that she wasn't lying to her best friend.

\* \* \*

Eve, Luke and Jess stared at the church from across the street a few minutes after curfew. Blue-and-white striped tents that looked like they came from a circus garage sale draped the old stone building.

'I guess the fumigation isn't done,' Luke said. 'But I don't see any guards.' He started across the street.

'Spoke too soon.' Eve caught him by the arm and pulled him back into the shadows. She nodded at someone in a hazmat suit walking towards the church from the rectory. 'What are we going to do? We could get by without the sword if we have to, but what if Mr Dokey really was telling you the bowl is in the church?'

'We have to check it out,' he answered.

'Want me to go all drama again, try to distract the guard?' Jess asked. 'I'm not sure I can do it as well as I did at the courthouse. The class – this whole day – has really taken it out of me.'

*She really does look wiped out*, Eve thought. *I hope she isn't getting— Not going there. Enough to worry about without that,* she told herself.

Luke narrowed his eyes and studied the church for a moment. 'I have an idea.'

Eve looked over at Jess. 'He has an idea.' Jess only managed a faint smile in response.

'Come on.' Luke led the way to the cemetery gate farthest away from the church. It gave a soft metallic creak as he swung it open.

'Perfect ending to a perfect day,' Jess commented as Luke waved her and Eve inside the graveyard.

'In some of those papers we found hidden in the church, there was a sketch that looked like a passage running from one of the mausolea to the crypt,' Luke explained as they picked their way through the old headstones. 'If there really is one, we should be able to use it to get inside without being seen. And the crypt is where the sword is, anyway. Start looking for a mausoleum that's shaped kinda like the White House rotunda.'

Eve snickered. 'You really are a history geek.'

'Come on,' Luke protested. 'Everybody knows what the White House rotunda looks like, unless those somebodies are so fashion-obsessed that they have no room in their brains for anything other than names of designers who make shoes that look like hooves and—'

'Alexander McQueen,' Eve and Jess said together. 'May he rest in peace,' Eve added.

It used to bug the hell out of Eve when Luke made fun of her for being a fashion head or acted like she was shallow. Now she thought it was kinda funny. Probably because, no matter how he felt about her romantically, Eve was sure Luke genuinely liked her. He'd become almost her second BFF in the short time he'd lived in town. Not that she saw him as a girl friend, obviously.

'Just please look for a mausoleum that is more round than square, OK?' Luke asked. 'I think there were ivy vines carved into the stone on the sides, or at least that's what it looked like in the drawing.'

Eve used the LED light on her keychain and Jess used her iPhone to light their way as they began their search. *I wonder if my power would let my fingers be LED lights*, Eve thought. She had the feeling that if she could just find the dimmer switch for her power, she could go from lightning bolts to those golden waves she'd used on the portal, to a gentle glow that could light her way.

The path they were walking down split in two directions. 'Which way should we try?' Eve asked, looking about. Her back felt itchy, like someone was watching her.

'Go right,' Luke answered. 'The children's section is to the left. No mausolea over there.'

'There's a whole section just for children?' Jess

asked sadly. She reached over and took Eve's hand as Luke nodded.

Eve took a quick glance to the left and saw something pale moving among the lambs and angels that dominated the children's part of the cemetery. The sight made her heart clench like a fist, a fist that only relaxed a little when she realized what the white form was – another guard.

'Hazmat over there anyway,' she whispered as they moved deeper into the adult section of the graveyard. Or was it actually Amunnic? The itchy sensation between her shoulder blades grew more insistent. She took another quick look at the figure in the hazmat suit. Not facing in their direction. *No one is watching you*, she told herself. *And if that was Amunnic, he'd be rushing over for some of your non-plague-infected blood.*

Eve took a shallow breath. The air felt thick, like there might be a storm later. Thick air was wrong. It didn't even seem possible for Eve to pull it into her lungs. 'There's a square one,' she said. It looked almost like a mini plantation house, with its rows of columns. She wondered who came up with the idea of mausolea in the first place. To her, they seemed a little goofy. And creepy. Definitely creepy. Spreepy, even.

'I think I might see it over there.' Luke picked up his pace. 'Yeah, that looks like the sketch I saw.' He stopped in front of a rounded stone structure with vines carved all around the entrance. There was an iron gate across the entrance, but when Luke pushed on it, it opened easily.

They all stepped inside. 'I don't get how there's a passage from in here to anywhere. There's only one gate – the one we just came through,' Eve said.

'If we're in the right place, one of these niches should be the entrance to the passage.' Luke walked to the far wall and began running his hands over the rectangles carved into the stone. They reminded Eve of big dresser drawers, but with no handles.

'Aren't there bodies sealed up behind those?' Jess asked. 'I saw this movie once where these guys decided to do a séance inside a place like this, and before I could close my eyes and bite the inside of my cheek to keep from screaming, some nasty rotten corpses came crawling out of the slots in the wall.'

'Most of the niches hold bodies, or will,' Luke answered. 'But not the one we're looking for.' He continued feeling his way along the wall. 'Yeah, here we go.' He pulled a large chunk of stone free, revealing a short, narrow tunnel. 'Who wants to go first?'

They all looked into the darkness of the gaping hole.

'I will,' Eve said. The tunnel was so narrow that she had to slide in on her belly and wiggle through. When she came out the other side, she was standing in a room not much bigger than an elevator. Across from her, a stone staircase splotched with moss led deeper down.

'You OK?' Luke called.

'Yeah. It's all clear over here,' Eve called back.

About three seconds later, Luke joined her. 'This is so cool.'

Eve stared at him.

'In a Hardy Boys kinda way. I told you I read them when I was a kid,' he confessed. 'This is like something out of one of those books.'

'Something just crunched under my knee,' Jess announced from inside the tunnel. 'I'm telling myself it was a really big potato chip. And not part of a skeleton.'

'The skeletons are in the other niches,' Luke told her. 'I'm pretty sure the one you're in has only been used as a passageway.'

'Good to know,' Jess muttered as she scrambled free.

'At least you two wore sensible clothes tonight,' Luke commented.

Sensible as in black, all the better to – hopefully – sneak up on Amunnic. But Eve was not happy that she'd chosen to wear her silk Da-Nang cargo pants. They now had a hole ripped in one thigh. And not an attractive, perfectly placed hole either. Just a ragged, ugly hole of a hole. Jess's high-waisted skinny pants hadn't made it through in much better shape. A layer of dust and grit had taken away their usual sheen.

'Sensible.' Jess snorted. 'He just called my once third-favourite pair of pants sensible.' Tired as she was, she still managed to work up some indignation.

'He didn't mean it,' Eve told her. 'Well, he did, but he actually thinks sensible is good.' She trained her LED light down the stairs. They were rough and uneven, and the number of spider webs made it seem like they hadn't been used in . . . ever.

'Shall we?' Luke asked, with exaggerated politeness.

'Let's,' Eve answered, imitating his formal tone.

Luke went first, Eve and Jess close behind him. Eve couldn't think of anything but the fact that the stairs were taking them deeper and deeper under the earth. Were there graves right on the other side of the wall? She couldn't stop herself from imagining the corpses inside turning restlessly, disturbed by the presence of the living.

She felt a hand brush against her, then finger bones digging into her flesh. 'Eve, something has me,' Jess whispered, voice trembling.

'Me too,' Eve answered.

'What?' Luke demanded. 'What's back there?'

'No, that's me. I have you,' Jess told Eve. She gave Eve's shirt a tug. 'But something really does have me. By the hair.' She let out a little whimper. 'Get it off me.'

'I don't see anything back there. I should have brought a real flashlight,' Luke muttered. 'The Hardy Boys always had a flashlight.'

Eve twisted round in the narrow tunnel, trying to figure out how to zap whatever had Jess without hurting her friend. She shone the LED light into the darkness and saw that Jess's hair had gotten snagged by a root that had worked its way between two of the stones.

'It's OK. It's nothing,' Eve told Jess. 'Just a root.' She reached over Jess's head and gently untangled the lock of hair.

'I can't stop shaking, even though I know it was nothing,' Jess admitted as they continued on.

'That's totally normal,' Eve said. She was sure it was

only the power she'd absorbed at the power plant that was keeping her feeling so steady.

'You've got to duck when you get to the bottom,' Luke told them. 'There's a doorway, but it's low.'

It wasn't just the doorway that was low. The tunnel that the doorway opened into was low too. They had to hunch over to walk down it.

'I guess this is a good place to get buried alive,' Jess commented. 'Since we're already in a cemetery and everything. Convenient.'

'No one's getting buried alive,' Luke said. A stream of gritty earth fell onto Eve's hair just as the words left his mouth, making them a lot less convincing.

'What's that smell?' Jess asked. To Eve, it was more of a taste than a smell. She felt as if she'd swallowed something oily and bitter.

'It must be the stuff they're fumigating with,' Luke guessed. 'That's gotta mean we're almost at the crypt in the church basement.'

The light from Jess's cell and Eve's LED showed the ground under their feet changing from earth to brick as they passed through another low doorway. 'There's a cemetery under the church?' Jess asked.

'Kind of,' Luke answered. 'The church was built over the oldest part of the cemetery. Most of the town's founding families are buried here.'

They straightened up as they entered the crypt. At least they were able to stand up in here. There was a cold damp musty smell as well as the smell of the fumigators. Gravestones had been laid on the floor and round the sides of the crypt, and there were large monuments and sarcophagi in the centre of the space. Eve guessed there were probably at least a hundred gravestones. 'Listen to this one,' she said, shining her light on one of the stones. '*Mary Abigail Hastings, faithful, virtuous and weary. Mother of eleven, survived by nine.*'

'Weary. Huh. I bet,' Jess said. 'Eleven kids.'

'The sword is under a big stone table. It has a bronze plaque set in the top,' Luke told them. 'I'm not sure if it's an elaborate headstone or some kind of memorial.'

'Lord Medway's stone!' Jess exclaimed. She aimed her cellphone light at a large, austere cross of black marble. His name and birth and death dates were carved so deeply they were still easy to read. There was nothing else on the marker. 'What an evil man. He invited demons into our town for his own gain. How could anyone do that?'

'I wonder if he's with the demons now,' Eve said.

'I wonder if they dragged him off to hell when he died.' The thought sent a chill through her, a chill too powerful for the hot electricity still inside her to combat.

'Wherever he is, it's only his body down here with us,' Luke answered.

As if in response, a yowl of anger seared the air, followed by a ferocious hissing.

'What the—' Luke exclaimed.

Eve tracked the sound with her LED and saw a cat staring at her, ears pressed tight against its head, mouth stretched open as if about to screech again.

'I am so not a cat person,' Luke muttered.

'Dogs all the way,' Jess agreed as the grey tabby leaped onto a headstone, then launched itself into the darkness.

'I think that might have been the same cat from the other night,' Luke said, peering after it.

*Or Amunnic.* The thought sneaked into Eve's brain. She didn't share it. What was the point? If it was the demon, it was gone, and she had no idea where. 'We have to remember that we're looking for the bowl too,' was all she said.

'Right. It wasn't in the tunnel. One of us would

have stepped on it,' Luke answered. 'Maybe we should spread out as we walk so we don't miss it.'

Eve reluctantly moved to the opposite side of the crypt and walked slowly, scanning the ground around her with every step. She jerked to a stop when she heard the sound of vomiting. Luke.

Did *he* have the plague now?

'Luke, are you OK?' Jess cried.

Eve rushed over to him. He reached out an arm, stopping her. 'Don't look,' he told her.

Too late. She'd already seen.

Briony lay on top of the stone table Luke had described. Her arms and legs were flung out. And she was pale, pale as skimmed milk. Lifeless. *She's been drained of blood*, Eve realized.

# Chapter Nine

Luke reached out and ran two fingers down Briony's cheek. It was cold; as cold as the slab of stone she lay on. He could hardly comprehend that she was the girl he'd gone out with, laughed with, even kissed once. He remembered how warm her lips had felt during the quick moment they were against his.

'I don't want to get used to seeing dead bodies,' Eve said softly, and Luke knew she was thinking of how they'd watched the life drain out of Payne on the night they fought the wargs.

'You won't,' Jess said. 'None of us will. It's not something that could ever become ordinary.'

'Will you take the sword?' Luke asked her. 'It's under the table.'

'Why aren't you going to—' Jess began.

He answered by sweeping Briony's body into his arms. As he cradled her against his chest, he felt her coldness begin to fill him. Eve put her hand on his arm, and that spot of warmth helped; it felt as if it could keep him calm.

'How will we explain this?' Eve asked after a moment.

'I don't know. But we can't leave her down here. She might never be found,' Luke answered. He couldn't deal with the idea of Briony's body abandoned in this old, sad graveyard that no one ever visited.

'Of course we can't,' Eve agreed.

Luke walked directly up into the church, Eve and Jess following him in silence, as if they were part of a funeral procession. If they were caught by the guards, so be it. He wasn't going to try to push Briony's body through the gap into the mausoleum. The thought of it repulsed him.

As he carried Briony past the altar, he said a silent prayer for her. He'd known that there was a chance they wouldn't find Amunnic's victims before the demon drained them. But he'd known it in his head. He realized that in his heart, he'd been deluding himself. He'd been so sure they would be able to kill Amunnic before he took a life.

The same way he'd been promising himself that they would kill the demon before his father or anyone else died from the plague. But this wasn't some movie. It wasn't a Hardy Boys mystery. There was no reason to believe the good guys would triumph. Briony's death proved that.

'Luke,' Eve said softly when they reached the church's main doors. 'There could be a guard out there. We need to figure out what we're going to say.'

She was right. All he'd been thinking about was getting Briony out of that horrible place. She'd looked like a human sacrifice laid out on that stone table. Forget *looked like*. That's exactly what she'd been. A human sacrificed to keep a demon alive.

'Well, I do live in the rectory,' Luke said. 'I guess we could have been going over there to get some of my stuff – since my dad's been moved to the plague ward and everything.'

'And you wanted to come into the church. You wanted a quiet place to think about your dad.'

'We all did,' Jess added, helping to fabricate the story. 'The guard must not have noticed us come in. We didn't even see a guard.'

'And Briony— We just found her in the church like this,' Luke said. 'That part's actually pretty much true.'

'I'll call an ambulance,' Eve said. Luke pushed open the door. Jess caught it and held it for him as he carried

Briony's body outside. Gently he laid her down on the grass to the side of the church. *Now she can see the stars at least*, he thought, even though that was nonsensical. Briony couldn't see anything, and never would again.

Rapid footfalls thudded towards them. 'No one's allowed in this area,' a guard in a hazmat suit called to them. 'And it's after curfew. You three should all be at home.'

Luke stepped to the side, allowing the guard to see Briony's body. 'We found her in the church. I'm the minister's son. I came to get some stuff from the rectory, then we decided to stop in the church for a minute.' He gulped. 'She was on the floor.' The lies came tumbling out with an ease that surprised him.

'We already called an ambulance,' Eve added.

'Get away from her. Right now!' the guard ordered. 'Most likely she's a plague victim and you have no protection. Go over to the sidewalk and put on masks.' He handed out three mouth masks, like the ones Eve's mother had given her.

Luke hated to leave Briony with a stranger, but he had no choice. He, Eve and Jess followed the guard's instructions, slipping on the masks as they stood and waited for the ambulance.

'Second time tonight,' Jess said as the ambulance's

flashing blue light appeared down the street. 'It feels like we just called them for Sean.' She sat down on the kerb, shoulders slumped with exhaustion.

'We pretty much did,' Eve answered. 'Get ready to be questioned. There's a police cruiser too.'

The second time Luke went through the story, it didn't come out so easily. When he told the police they'd found Briony's body in the church, it was almost like he was back in the crypt, finding her again, feeling her stiffness and coldness as he lifted her into his arms. His voice broke, and he had to pause and swallow hard a couple of times before he could continue. Jess began to cry as he spoke, and Eve wrapped her arms tightly around herself, as if she was afraid she was about to shatter.

'I have enough for now,' the cop said when Luke had given him the basic details. 'I want to get you three home. It's after curfew. Your parents are going to be looking for you.' He opened the back door to the cruiser, and Luke, Eve and Jess climbed in.

There was no way they'd be able to sneak back out later that night. Which meant Amunnic would have all those hours to feed uninterrupted. The realization sickened Luke. Would the demon drain another victim dry before dawn?

*Jess, you look like fresh death.* Eve had to clench her teeth together to keep those horrible words from spilling out when she arrived at Jess's house the next morning. Against her pale, pale face, Jess's blush and lipstick looked as bright and garish as clown make-up, and her eyes had none of their usual brightness or sparkle.

'Where's Luke?' Jess asked. 'We need to get to work.'

'We do,' Eve agreed. 'And we will. He just thought maybe we needed a little girl time first. I know seeing Seth was so horrible.'

Jess nodded. 'Finding Briony too. Is Luke OK? Are you?'

'As OK as we can be,' Eve answered.

'I need some juice,' Jess said. 'I don't really feel like eating, but my throat is all dry. Want some? Or wait – it's a hot chocolate day, isn't it?'

'It's a hot chocolate week,' Eve told her, and they headed for the kitchen.

'Oh my God, Peter. It's not even ten-thirty and you're eating ice cream?' Jess exclaimed. Her younger brother sat at the table eating Cherry Garcia straight out of the carton.

'Have to,' Peter said. 'What if the power goes out

again?' He continued stuffing the ice cream into his mouth.

'Whatever.' Jess went over to the pantry, which contained pretty much every kind of snack food ever invented, and pulled out a can of Abuelita Mexican chocolate. Yum. Hot chocolate was the best thing when you were upset. But Mexican hot chocolate, all cinnamony and dark, was the best thing *ever*.

'Hot chocolate? When it's already ninety degrees out? And you act like I'm the crazy one.' Peter gave an exaggerated shake of his head.

Eve sat down next to him. Glossy travel brochures were piled in the centre of the table. Their mothers had decided to plan a double family vacation for that summer. It was months away, but they thought everybody needed something happy to think about with all the awful things that had been happening in Deepdene.

'Peter!' Jess's mom appeared in the doorway. 'Need your help.' Her voice was still thick with sleep. She flapped her hand at him. 'Store. Now.'

'Fine, fine.' Peter grabbed his ice cream and spoon and ambled out of the kitchen, pausing to give Eve a noogie on the top of her head.

'Oh, wait!' Jess called. 'Mom, you forgot your purse.

You're not going to get far without the car keys.'

Mrs Meredith walked back into the kitchen, a little unsteadily. 'Oh, yes.' It was sitting on the counter about a foot away from where she was standing, but she didn't seem to see it. Eve picked it up and handed it to her. Mrs Meredith closed her fist around the strap instead of looping it over her shoulder, then left the room without saying goodbye.

'I hope my mom's not getting sick too,' Jess said. 'She's acting a little weird, don't you think?'

Eve agreed, but she didn't want to freak Jess out. It had been bad enough when Seth came down with the plague. 'Maybe a little,' she said, keeping her voice casual. 'But she probably hasn't been getting enough sleep. I know my mom hasn't. She's pulling insane hours at the clinic, but when she's home, she can't relax at all. She just paces around.'

Jess put milk in a saucepan to heat. 'So, how's it going having Luke at your house all the time. Is it—'

The doorbell rang, interrupting her. 'I'm here,' Luke called. 'Should I just come in?'

'Sure. We're in the kitchen,' Jess replied.

'Tell you later,' Eve answered. Her gaze snagged on one of the brochures. 'This would be awesome,' she told Jess. 'Villa in Praiano. Breathtaking view of the

Amalfi coast. Terrace. Private beach. Pizza oven. And you know we could convince our parents to let us take at least a weekend in Paris.'

'Wow, it's genetic,' Luke said, ignoring the fact that Eve was ignoring him. 'I just left your moms at Eve's house doing exactly the same thing. They seemed to be leaning towards Argentina, though. Something about the wineries.'

'Huh?' Eve asked.

'Just now?' Jess said, brow furrowing.

'Yeah. They told me they'd decided to spend a half an hour planning a vacation, with no talking about the plague allowed. Seemed like a good idea,' he answered.

'But . . .' Jess started.

'It wasn't Jess's mom. She just left,' Eve said.

'I know Jess's mother,' Luke argued. 'It was . . .' His words trailed off.

Eve felt the blood drain from her face. 'Jess's mom couldn't be in two places at once.'

Jess grabbed the phone and dialled. 'Hi, Mrs Evergold,' she said, voice shaky. 'Is my mom there? I need to talk to her for a sec.'

Eve and Luke didn't take their eyes off Jess as she continued talking. 'Mom, did you know you left your purse on the kitchen counter?' Jess listened for a minute. 'Oh, OK. See you in a while, then.'

She put down the phone and stared into space for a moment.

'Jess?' Eve pressed.

'My mom said she didn't bother to take her purse. She just stopped in at your place when she was doing her morning jog. She always jogs when she's stressed out,' Jess said in a monotone. 'She sounded totally normal. She even said, "Bye, sweetie-pie," at the end. That's what she does every time we talk on the phone.'

Eve flashed on how strange Mrs Meredith had seemed in the kitchen a few minutes ago. She hadn't said goodbye. And she'd picked up her purse as if she'd never even held one before. 'I can't believe it. Amunnic was right here in the kitchen with us.'

'But why?' Luke said. 'He just took on the appearance of Jess's mother in order to walk around for a minute and then leave? Why didn't he attack?'

Jess's eyes widened with horror. 'Peter. He took Peter with him!'

Eve's blood ran cold. It was true. The demon had Jess's little brother!

# Chapter Ten

Eve, Jess and Luke ran out of the house. 'Peter!' Luke shouted. Jess and Luke were shouting Peter's name too, and Luke could hear Jess's voice shaking with fear.

'How long ago did Amunnic leave with him?' Luke asked as they hurried down to the sidewalk.

'Not even five minutes,' Eve said. 'Maybe only two.' She scanned the street. A hazmat-suited person was cordoning off the house on the other side of the Christies', but other than that no one else was in sight.

'Even if it was just two minutes, they're gone. And we have no idea where!' Jess cried.

'They didn't take the car,' Eve pointed out. 'Let's just go to the end of the block at least and see if we can spot them.' Luke took off running almost before the words were out of her mouth, with Eve and Jess only a few steps behind.

But Medway Lane was deserted. There wasn't even another CDC agent in sight.

'It's going to kill Peter!' Jess screamed. 'It's going to kill him!'

Luke gave Jess a hug. He could tell she needed one. He could feel tremors running through her frame. 'It's not. We have time, remember?' Luke didn't mention that they had time because Amunnic would be slowly drinking Peter's blood. 'We're going to find him.'

Jess pulled away. 'How? We have no idea where he is.'

'We were close last night,' Luke reminded her. 'Amunnic had been in the crypt. We wouldn't have found Briony there otherwise.'

'How does that help us now?' Jess's voice was nearly a shriek. Luke could tell she was teetering on the edge of all-out hysteria.

'It eliminates one place, for starters,' Eve told her. 'And we already eliminated the power plant. We just have to figure out the other spots that Amunnic might use to take his victims.' Too late, she wished she hadn't used the word victim. But that's what Peter and the others were, and Eve, Jess and Luke all knew it.

'Amunnic has a lot of people now. That means he needs space,' Luke said.

'Mr Dokey said *you* knew where the bowl was,' Eve reminded him.

'Right. That means it has to be a place he knows I know, a place I'd think of,' Luke answered. *So where? Where, where, where?* 'I'm such an idiot!' he exclaimed as the answer came to him. 'I'm in Mr Dokey's history class. He'd been showing us stuff he brought back from Egypt just before he got sick, and he kept teasing us, saying he was saving something really cool for last. He was talking about the bowl! Has to be! I don't know why I thought he was telling me the bowl was at the church.'

'The bowl's at the school!' Eve cried. 'And that's where Amunnic has been taking everyone he grabs. The closed school. The big, now *empty* school. It makes total sense.'

*It should have been the first place we searched,* Luke thought. Definitely before the power plant. The school would be the perfect place for Amunnic to take his victims. He'd probably had Briony there too, and just moved her body to the crypt after she died. The crypt was the perfect place to hide the dead.

'I can't believe we didn't think of that!' Jess exclaimed.

'I can't either,' Luke said.

Jess started to run again. Eve and Luke caught up to her seconds later. It wasn't hard. Jess was usually crazy fast, but today she was slowing down and panting after just those few steps.

*Don't be too late. Don't be too late. Don't be too late.* The words repeated themselves over and over along with the thudding of Luke's heart as they reached the football field. He skidded to a stop in front of the broken window of the boys' locker room. He flung it open, then took Eve by the waist and swung her inside. He couldn't believe his body reacted to her in the middle of a life-and-death situation, but it did.

'Hurry,' Jess begged. Luke helped her through the window, then scrambled through himself. Immediately, he pulled the sword free from the scabbard he wore strapped to his back under his shirt.

Eve moved into the lead position as they hurried through the locker room. It always felt wrong to Luke not to be between her and danger, but she had her powers, and she needed a clear shot to use them.

She cracked open the door and looked out into the hallway. 'Empty,' she whispered, then, moving silently, stepped out of the locker room. One of Luke's sneakers squeaked on the smooth wooden floor as he followed her.

He winced, but didn't hear any movement from deeper in the school. Was this going to turn out to be another dead end? It seemed like the perfect place, but the building felt deserted, completely different from a regular day with lockers banging, kids racing to make it to class, and teachers yelling at kids not to run.

When they entered Mr Dokey's room it felt completely different too. Mr Dokey was one of those teachers who kept things lively in his class. The guy hardly ever stood still. When he lectured, he paced up and down the aisles between the desks, hands gesturing constantly as he spoke. Luke had never experienced Mr Dokey's room when it was quiet.

'The stuff he brought back from his trip to Egypt is over here.' Luke's voice sounded loud, even though he was speaking more softly than he usually did. He walked over to the bookshelf to the right of the chalkboard. 'Not here,' he said more softly. The closest thing was an engraved bronze pot that held kohl for blackening the eyelids and lashes. Not even close to the picture they'd seen of the ceramic bowl Amunnic used to catch his victims' blood, the bowl the magician had later imprisoned the demon in.

'You said he was showing you the stuff a little at a

time, and that he was saving the best for last,' Eve reminded him. 'Let's check the closet.'

It was a good idea. But the bowl wasn't there, only maps, textbooks, paper, just usual school stuff. 'Mr Dokey wouldn't have said I knew where it was if it was at his house. That doesn't make sense. School makes sense.' Luke thought for a moment. Where would Dokey keep the bowl if not in his classroom?

'We should check the teachers' lounge,' Jess said. She still sounded a little breathless from the run, although Luke and Eve had managed to catch their breath.

'Teachers' lounge. Yeah,' Luke agreed. They hurried out of Mr Dokey's room and down the hall to the lounge – then hesitated. It was just an automatic thing. Kids didn't go in there. It was strictly teachers only.

Eve gave a nervous giggle. 'I can't believe I'm OK with hunting a demon, but feel weird about going in here.' She grabbed the doorknob and swung open the door.

'This is it?' Luke asked, taking in the conference table and chairs, the coffee maker, the fridge and the leather couch. He shook his head, smiling a little at his reaction. 'I don't know what I was expecting.'

'A pool table at least,' Eve answered. 'There are even rumours of a hot tub!' She opened the bathroom door. 'Nope. Not even a shower. Just your basic sink.'

Jess sank down in the closest chair. 'The bowl's not here.'

'We don't know that for sure.' Luke started opening the cupboards over the microwave and coffee maker – nothing but napkins, stained coffee mugs, and little packets of sugar and sweetener.

'I guess we do now,' Eve commented. 'There aren't many places in here it could be hiding. Do you think he would have left it in the principal's office for safekeeping?'

'Possible, I guess,' Luke answered. 'We might as well look since—' His cell rang, the Ludacris ringtone sounding insanely out of place. A mix of hope and nauseating fear rolled through him when he saw the call was from his dad's cell. 'Hello?' he said, anxious and eager.

'Luke. Need you,' his dad croaked.

'What's wrong?' Luke burst out.

'I need you.'

'I'm there,' Luke promised. 'Just hang on.' He hung up and jammed his cell back in his pocket. 'It's my dad,' he told Eve and Jess. 'I don't know. He sounded dreadful. I have to get over there. When my mom— I didn't get to say goodbye. I have to get over there.'

'Of course you do,' Eve told him. 'Go.'

'But Amunnic,' Luke said.

'Go,' Eve told him again. 'Jess and I will keep looking for the bowl and Amunnic. Your dad's more important.'

'But—' Luke hesitated. He knew finding the demon and killing him could save his father and everyone else in the plague ward. But his father wanted him. If he died before— 'OK, I'm gone. Call me if you find something.' He bolted without waiting for an answer.

His dad had sounded horrible. Barely hanging on. Luke had to get to him before— He had to get to him while— Luke had to get to his father. Period.

'I need to rest. Just for a sec.' Jess leaned against the wall and slid down it until she was sitting on the floor outside the girls' locker room. They'd searched it after they'd checked the principal's office. No bowl – or any other sign of Amunnic – in either place.

'Are you OK?' Eve asked. She didn't know why – it was so obvious Jess was anything *but* OK. 'Do you want some water, maybe? Or do you want to go home and rest for a while? I can keep loo—'

Jess shook her head. 'I'm not going home without Peter.'

'Me neither,' Eve promised.

Jess wrapped her hand around Eve's ankle. 'Eve! Look down there.'

Eve followed Jess's gaze and frowned. 'I'm not sure what I'm looking for?'

'On the ground. A little past the drinking fountain. I think that's my mom's purse!' Jess cried. She used both hands to shove herself to her feet. She stumbled down the hall, Eve at her side.

'I was right!' Jess swooped down and snatched up the bag. 'She – I mean, Amunnic – had this when he left with Peter!'

That meant the demon was here. Somewhere in the school with them. It was go time. Time to end this.

Jess's eyes glittered with a feverish determination. 'That demon is going to be very sorry he chose my brother to mess with. I know I've only had a few kung fu lessons, but I'm going to release every bit of hi-yah I have on Amunnic!'

# Chapter Eleven

'Peter's lucky to have you for a sister,' Eve told Jess. 'Let's finish this. I bet Amunnic is holding everyone in the basement. He dropped the purse right in front of the door that goes down there.' She tapped the DO NOT ENTER sign on the door. 'I guess we're going to get the chance to see every forbidden area in this place before we're done.'

'Let's go get my brother.' Jess opened the door, her hand shaking.

'Me first,' Eve whispered. She slid in front of Jess and started down the flight of plain cement stairs. Jess followed her. There was another door at the bottom. Eve swung it open, and tried to look every-where at once.

Her eyes almost immediately snagged on Peter, tied to a chair near the centre of the big, dimly lit, dusty room. Rose, Leo and Cathy were tied to chairs on one side of Peter; Dave and Elisha to chairs on the other. They all looked up, stunned.

*Where was the demon?* Amunnic was nowhere in sight.

'Oh God, Peter!' Jess cried, and Eve looked back over at him. She knew what Amunnic did to his victims, how he fed, but it was still almost impossible to accept what she was seeing. The ceramic bowl rested under Peter's right arm. A fast, narrow stream of blood flowed from a puncture wound just above his wrist into the bowl, blood for the demon to drink. The others each had a similar puncture wound in the same place.

Jess stumbled across the room to Peter and began to untie him. Eve hurried to Rose's side and started working on her bindings.

'We all have to get out of here before that psycho comes back,' Dave cried. 'He's coming back. He'll want to drink that blood while it's fresh.'

'We will. We are,' Eve told him.

Rose didn't say anything as Eve freed her hands and went to work on her feet. Rose's eyelids were only partway open, and through the slits, all Eve could see was white. Her eyes had rolled back in her head.

'You're OK,' Eve murmured. 'We're going to get you

out of here.' She didn't get a response. She was afraid Rose had lost consciousness. How much blood had Amunnic taken from her? Her skin was cool under Eve's fingers as she worked on the knots. 'How long has she been this out of it?' she asked.

Out of the corner of her eye, Eve saw Cathy turn her head towards them. 'Since I got here,' she answered. 'He drank more blood from her than anyone.'

'Except Briony, and she's dead,' Leo added. While Cathy's voice had been ragged with fear, Leo's was flat. *He's gone through so much, he can't feel anything any more*, Eve realized.

Rose began to slide off the chair as Eve undid the last knot. Eve reached out and guided her down to the ground, making sure her head didn't hit the cement floor.

'Eve, help me with Peter!' Jess cried. 'I can't get him free. My hands keep slipping.' She held them up to Eve, and Eve could see her fingers were slick with Peter's blood.

'Hey, Peter, hey, buddy,' Eve said as she joined Jess by his side. 'We're going to get you out of here.' She looked over at Jess. 'We need to stop that bleeding.'

'Where am I?' Peter asked, as if seeing Eve and Jess for the first time.

'You're at school, sweetie,' Jess said. Eve didn't think she'd ever heard Jess call her little brother 'sweetie' before. 'At the high school.'

Peter looked around, brow furrowed. 'This isn't the high school,' he said. 'How'd I even get here?'

*He's in shock,* Eve decided. She managed to free his hands and started to work on his feet.

'Later,' Jess said. 'I'll explain everything later.' She grabbed the ruffle cascading across the front of her halter top – one of the ten items of clothing she had on the list of what to save in the event of a fire – in both hands and gave it a vicious yank, then wrapped the strip of silk chiffon around Peter's arm, pulling it tight across his wound.

How *were* they going to explain what had happened? Eve wondered. Not important, she thought. Not now, at least.

'This isn't working!' Jess burst out. Eve looked at the makeshift bandage. Blood had already soaked through it.

Jess pulled off her woven belt, hands trembling. 'Maybe it needs a tourniquet.'

'What he needs is a paramedic,' Eve answered. 'I

should have called the ambulance the second we got down here. We need help to get everybody out before the demon comes back.'

'Demon?' Cathy cried. Elisha began to whimper.

'Demon sounds right to me,' Leo said, his voice still stripped of all emotion.

'We don't have time to wait for help,' Jess protested. 'It could be back any second.'

'I know. But there are too many of them,' Eve answered. 'And you're . . . you're not feeling well, Jess.'

Jess opened her mouth to protest. 'You know it's true,' Eve said before Jess could get out a word. 'Any day that I can run faster than you – the way I did when we were cutting across the field – is a day you're sick. But it's OK. It's all going to be over soon. You'll be fine.'

Eve whipped her cell out of her bag. 'No bars,' she announced. 'I'll go upstairs.' Jess nodded as she wound her belt around Peter's upper arm. As she took the stairs two and three at a time, Eve could hear her best friend talking in a soothing voice.

She checked her cell again when she reached the hallway. Three beautiful bars. Just as she started to punch in 911, Luke's father came round the corner. All the air left Eve's lungs in a *whoosh*. Reverend

Thompson was carrying Luke in his arms! Luke hung there, body limp, head lolling.

'What happened?' she shouted as the reverend walked towards her. 'Is he OK? Don't bring him this way. There's a demon. It'll be coming back here. You have to get Luke out and call for help! There are six people down there. They've all lost blood. One of them is—'

Eve felt her heart drop into her stomach as the truth hit her. That wasn't Reverend Thompson, not with his lip curling into a snarl. It was Amunnic! Many Faces. And it had Luke! That phone call from his *father* had been a fake, a trap.

'You evil bastard!' she screamed. Her fury got her power churning, hot and strong. She could almost see it glowing through her skin. But she couldn't attack. She couldn't risk it. Not with Luke in the demon's arms.

Seeing her hesitate, Amunnic laughed, a sound like two pieces of sandpaper rubbing together. That laugh coming out of a being with the Reverend Thompson's face and body was sacrilege.

Eve suddenly heard Master Justin's voice in her head. *Side kick!* OK, she'd only had one lesson of kung fu, but if she could just get Amunnic to drop

Luke . . . One, two – and three! She spun and kicked out, aiming for Amunnic's knee.

Satisfaction rocketed through her, almost as hot and bright as her power, when she heard the demon give a grunt of pain. Without hesitating, she landed another kick in the same spot.

Amunnic gave a growl of fury, then turned and threw Luke through the open doorway leading to the basement. Eve's bones tingled with sympathy pain as she heard his body tumbling down the cement stairs.

'Luke!' she heard Jess cry from the basement. 'Oh God, Luke!'

'That was one huge mistake!' she yelled at Amunnic as the demon lunged for her, arms outstretched. 'No one treats my friends that way.' She thrust out her hands, aiming at Amunnic's belly. Lightning bolts flew out of her fingers, one after the other – so fast and hot they smoked and sparked.

But Amunnic crouched down like a line backer, ducking the bolts. He twisted his body, and rammed himself into Eve, shoulder first. She flew backwards, smashing against the wall behind her. Some of her bolts had hit him – she could smell the stench of burning hair, and a smoking bald spot had appeared on the side of Amunnic's head. But most of the dozens and dozens of bolts had missed the mark. They'd sped over Amunnic's head and crashed into the window at the far end of the hall, smashing it to sparkling bits of glass.

The demon prepared to ram her again. If he hit her while her back was still pressed against the wall, that was it. Her spine would snap. At least Amunnic was clumsy in his human form, clumsy and not nearly as fast as Eve.

She twisted her body to the side an instant before he rammed her, and he ended up hurling himself into the wall instead. The plaster cracked as his body hit.

Eve sprang a few steps away, raised her hands, and fired. The demon dropped to his knees, a move that was awkward, but effective. One of his shirt sleeves began to smoulder, but most of her bolts had missed again.

She let more zaps free as Amunnic shoved himself to his feet. *He's so strong*, she thought as he kept advancing on her even as her power struck him in the same shoulder again, then the chest and the belly.

Amunnic snatched one of her outstretched hands while she was still blasting and used it to jerk her to him. The bolts from her free hand went wild, hitting the lockers with a metallic sizzling and the scent of melting paint. He pinned both arms to her sides.

In this position, she couldn't use her power against him. She was facing the wrong way. *OK, OK. Master Justin went over this, remember?* she thought. He'd used the last twenty minutes of class to demonstrate a few self-defence moves.

She raised her elbow up, twisted towards Amunnic, and brought it down on his arms. She wrapped her fist around her hand, then used the force of both arms to jerk her elbow up into the demon's chin. *And tiger claw*, she thought, raking her nails across Amunnic's face, straight across the eyes.

It worked! She'd broken free! She owed Master Justin a muffin basket. Or some fancy nunchucks.

The demon recovered quickly, so quickly she only had the chance to fire a few bolts. He lurched at her and gave her a one-armed shove that sent her back through the doorway leading to the stairs. She had a sickening moment when she knew she was going to fall, but couldn't stop it.

She pinwheeled her arms, trying to catch her balance. Too late. She was falling, her head and back bouncing on the hard steps as she hurtled down.

The demon started down the stairs after her.

'It's Amunnic!' Eve yelled, and before the demon

could reach her, Jess launched herself at him with a screech of outrage.

'Jess, no!' Peter shouted. But Jess didn't hesitate. She leaped over her friend towards Amunnic, sweeping out with one leg. Her leg smashed into one of the demon's knees – the same knee Eve had managed to hit twice.

Eve's head was spinning too badly for her to stand up. But that didn't mean she couldn't zap. She tried to position her hands to let more of her bolts fly, but she couldn't find a way where she'd be sure she wouldn't accidentally hit Jess.

'Get away from him!' Peter yelled.

'He's stronger when he drinks, and it hasn't been that long. He's going to kill you!' Dave screamed. Elisha began to wail hysterically.

'You drank my brother's blood,' Jess screamed at the demon. 'I'm the one who'll be doing the killing.' She spun round and sent her elbow flying into the demon's gut, then she slammed one of her feet down on Amunnic's instep.

Eve could hear Jess's laboured pants. She could see the sweat gluing her shirt to her body. 'Jess, please, just get out of the way,' she cried. She could tell her friend had almost no strength left.

Jess ignored Eve, aiming another elbow blow at Amunnic. The demon gave a low, impatient growl and backhanded Jess. It was a small motion, but it sent Jess hurtling towards the wall. She hit it with a horrifying crunch, slithered into a heap on the floor, and lay still. Peter gave a howl of outrage.

'Nooo!' Eve slammed her power at the demon, using all her fury over what Amunnic had done to Jess, and to Luke, and to Peter, and to Leo and Cathy, to Briony, and Rose, and Dave and Elisha and to the whole town. Her bolt hit him full in the face.

The demon's eyes flashed red, losing the hazel colour of Reverend Thompson's. The skin on his face began to ripple, and dark patches of necrosis appeared. His nose almost disappeared into his head, and his lips curled back, revealing a double row of teeth. Amunnic's body stretched out and out, his arms and legs extending until they were impossibly long, and impossibly thin, his torso narrowing too.

One of the victims screamed, a long, high sound that a human shouldn't have been able to produce. Terror jolted through Eve. Instinctively she opened herself to the power around her. The lights dimmed as she sucked the electrical current into her, just as she had in the power plant.

Amunnic calmly stepped towards her, and Eve realized that with the power rushing into her body, she was momentarily unable to move. The demon raised one foot, and used it to grind Eve's right hand into the floor. He kept his weight there, pinning her, then used his free foot to kick her in the head. For a moment red squiggles filled her field of vision. Then everything went dark.

# Chapter Twelve

Eve felt something cold and rough under her cheek. She opened her eyes, and saw the cement floor of the school basement. Her head felt like it was throbbing in sync with her heartbeat as a memory rush reminded her what had happened. Amunnic had kicked her in the temple, and she'd passed out.

She tried to scramble up – but a wave of nausea had her sitting back down.

'He got us all,' she heard someone say.

Luke! Eve turned towards his voice and saw him tied to a chair along with the others. Joy and fear battled inside her: joy that he was alive, right there in front of her, fear that she wouldn't be able to save him – any of them. 'Where is he?' Eve cried.

'He left as soon as he got Peter set up again,' Luke answered. 'I heard the door lock behind us.'

Eve whipped her head towards Peter, taking in the

fact that his bandage and tourniquet were gone and his blood was again flowing into the ceramic bowl. 'Don't worry, Peter. It's OK. I'm getting you out of here.'

Peter's eyes didn't move from the door. 'Its eyes were red. Red.' *He's in deeper shock than before*, Eve realized. They all were. Leo's face was completely blank. Cathy had her eyes squeezed shut and was repeating 'not real' over and over. Elisha's whimpers had turned to small animal-like squeaks of pure fear. Rose – Rose was still slumped on the floor. Jess too. The demon hadn't bothered to tie her up.

'Not much time before he's back, I don't think,' Luke said.

His voice – his beautiful Luke-is-alive voice – spurred Eve into action. The fire fizzing through her veins reminded her that she had recharged. That moment when she'd been absorbing the energy had given him the chance to knock her out, but it had also filled her with new strength and power. She felt like a nuclear weapon.

Eve crawled over to Jess and gently, so, so gently, shook her by the shoulder. Jess gave a little moan, and her eyelids fluttered briefly, but didn't open all the way. Eve could feel that heat coming off her. She had a fever. She had it . . . the plague. That's probably why Amunnic hadn't bothered to tie her up. He probably had no interest in her since the plague had made her blood undrinkable.

An image of her friend's beautiful face ravaged by necrosis filled Eve's mind. *You're killing the demon,* she reminded herself. *No demon, no need for the plague warning, no harm to Jess. She'd get better – she had to.*

'Was lightning coming out of your hands?' Peter asked, in almost the same tone as he'd asked where he was.

'I don't think so,' Eve told him.

'The lighting came from the other thing,' Dave said. 'What the hell was it? It . . . it morphed. Its skin . . .' His words trailed off.

'We can talk about all of this when we're out of here,' Eve said. She figured she could probably zap the door lock hard enough to break it. But first she had to get everyone untied. She started with Luke.

'I can't believe I fell for that call,' he said as she worked on the knots around his wrists. 'How stupid was that? I'd barely walked out the front door when Amunnic grabbed me and smashed me over the head with something. Rock, maybe. Next thing I know, I'm tied up down here. I should never have gone.'

'It wasn't stupid. It was your dad. You thought it was your dad,' Eve answered. 'Of course you went.'

'Is Jess OK?' Peter asked, as if he'd just realized his sister was on the floor.

It was like his voice suddenly pulled Jess back to consciousness. 'Peter?' She slowly sat up. Her brow furrowed. 'You OK?'

Peter looked down at the bowl filling with his blood, and in a complete Peter move he actually grinned. 'I'm good,' he told his sister. 'That was one impressive combo you threw at that thing.' Eve could tell it took him a huge amount of effort to put on the show for Jess.

'But you forgot the "Hi-yah!"' Luke commented, gently teasing.

'I did!' Jess exclaimed. 'Crucial part.' She raised her hand to brush her hair away from her face, and froze. 'Look,' she finally said, turning her palm towards Eve. A dark, greasy spot of necrosis had bloomed near the centre of her hand. Tears flooded Jess's eyes.

'No, no, it's a good thing,' Eve told her. 'He'll leave you alone now.'

Jess nodded.

'So how long was I knocked out? How much time until we think he comes back?' Eve asked.

'You were only out maybe five minutes, I think,' Dave said.

'It won't be long until it's back,' Cathy put in. 'It never is. You've got to get us out of here!'

'On it!' Eve freed Luke's hands, and he immediately began working on the rope that held his feet to the chair. Jess had managed to slide over in front of Peter and was working on his ties, even though her hands were shaking almost uncontrollably.

Eve moved over next to her to help. 'Dave, do you think you're strong enough to carry Rose when everyone's untied?' she asked. 'There's no way she can walk.'

'Yeah, yeah, I can do that,' Dave answered.

'He's going to come back before you have us all free,' Leo predicted. He didn't sound concerned. That's how deep his shock and fright went. He was completely numbed out.

'I can help Jess,' Luke said. 'Can the others make it on their own?'

'Doubtful. At least not Leo and Cathy. Have you guys even had any food or water?' Eve asked Dave.

'He has this bucket he lets us drink out of, and Cathy told me he brings food once a day,' Dave answered.

'So it might take two trips to get everyone out once I blow the lock on the door,' Eve answered, trying to sound calm. 'Since we have a lot of people who need help.'

'Too late,' Leo said. 'I hear him.'

Eve listened for a moment, and heard a shuffling, scraping sound coming from the direction of the door.

'Maybe I can be a decoy,' Luke said, fast and low, as he finished untying himself. 'As soon as the door opens, I can make a run for it. Maybe Amunnic will chase me, and the rest of you could escape while I keep him busy.' Of course Luke would come up with a plan that put him in the most danger. Eve felt a rush of respect for him.

'Amunnic. You know that thing's name?' Peter sounded very confused.

'Long story,' Jess said.

'Back to the plan. If anyone's going to act like a decoy, it's going to be me,' Eve declared. She was the Deepdene Witch. A demon in her town was ultimately her responsibility.

'I should be the decoy,' Jess insisted. 'I'm faster than either of you. I'm in cheerleader-slash-kung-fu-student shape.'

'On a usual day, yes, yes you are,' Eve told her. 'But today—'

The sound of a creaky door swinging open interrupted her. Eve let herself fall back to the ground. It would give her an advantage if Amunnic thought she was still out. Jess followed her lead, lying back down too.

Luke had decided to act like he was still tied up. Through slitted eyes, Eve had seen him get back in the chair and lightly wrap the rope around his wrists.

Amunnic moved closer to Peter, and Peter let out a yip of panic. The demon ignored him. He slid the bowl from below Peter's arm to a spot underneath Luke's. Eve saw a long, wickedly sharp claw slide out of one of the demon's thin fingers.

*Not going to happen*, Eve thought. She quietly sprang to her feet. Amunnic must have caught the motion in his peripheral vision. He whirled to face her, red eyes glistening.

Eve flung out her hands, and her bolts flew out of her fingers as fast as arrows. Amunnic quickly bent his long, thin, rubbery body into a backbend, the top of his head brushing the floor behind him, allowing Eve's lightning to zing over him.

Almost as fast as one of her bolts, Amunnic

straightened up. He whipped out one of his impossibly long arms and caught her by the throat. Eve jammed her hands into his stomach and shoved her power directly into him.

The demon howled and tightened his grip. Eve began to choke, but kept hurling her volcanic power into him. The scent of burning flesh filled the room.

Amunnic squeezed harder. She could feel that hideous claw of his pierce her skin, and a moment later, blood began to run down her neck. It felt as if her power was flowing out with it.

Eve ground her teeth together, willing volt after volt into Amunnic. Suddenly his grip loosened. His eyes rolled up in his head, and he began to morph, his face and body bulging and contracting as they took on new appearances. For a fraction of a second, he looked like Jess's mother, then Luke's father. His body contorted again, and grey-and-white fur sprouted over his face.

*The cat!* Eve realized. *He took on the form of the cat!*

Faster and faster he cycled through his many faces, all the faces he'd used over the centuries. Eve recognized the homeless man, Mr Enslow, Phillip and her English teacher. How many times had she walked past the demon without recognizing him? All these people he'd disguised himself as so he could capture her friends and bring them down here.

Amunnic's faces changed even more rapidly, too fast for Eve's eyes to register more than a blur. Then with a *whomp* he ignited and let go of her. Flames covered every inch of his long body. Eve threw herself away from the searing heat.

And then it was over. The flames went out as quickly as they'd started. When they did, all that was left of Amunnic was a pile of coarse black ash on the floor.

# Chapter Thirteen

Eve looked down at Jess as she lay on the stretcher, waiting to be loaded into an ambulance. 'And the fun never stops,' Jess joked weakly.

'Never,' Luke agreed from his spot close to Eve's side.

Jess held her palm up to them, so they could see again that the spot of necrosis was gone. The puncture wounds on Amunnic's other victims had almost disappeared too, leaving only small pink marks behind after the demon turned to ash.

An EMT worker in a hazmat suit walked over to them. 'Lucky you forgot your cellphone in your locker,' she said to Luke. 'If you two hadn't come look-ing for it . . . well, it might have gone really differently for the other kids.'

Luke had improvised a story about needing his cell and realizing it was in his school locker. He said Eve had come with him to retrieve it and they'd heard moaning in the basement and gone down to check it out.

Dave had jumped in and said that they'd been partying down there, then they'd all gotten sick and ended up too weak to leave. He almost seemed to believe the story himself. Why wouldn't he? It was a lot less scary that the truth – that a demon had been drinking his blood.

'You're going to be fine,' another EMT worker said as he joined the group by Jess's stretcher. 'I was just on the radio with the plague centre. The new antibiotics seem to be working – and fast. The most recent victims are even asking to go home.'

'Hear that, Jess?' Eve asked. 'You're going to be fine.'

'Already am, thanks to you,' Jess answered. She grinned. 'I guess you'll keep coming to kung fu with me,' she said.

'You know it,' Eve answered.

'Am I invited?' Luke asked.

'Mmm. Maybe. If you're nice,' Eve told him.

'Luke's always nice,' Jess said pointedly as the EMTs began to roll her stretcher towards the ambulance.

'I can't wait to go over to the courthouse and see my dad. The real one,' Luke told Eve.

'I bet,' she answered. 'I just have one thing I need to do here. Will you stay with me?'

'The always-nice Luke Thompson? Of course,' he replied.

Eve led the way back down to the basement. 'I don't feel safe with this just lying around.' She touched the pile of ash with the very tip of her shoe.

Luke walked over to the bowl and picked it up. 'Let's put him back in here,' he suggested. 'This kept him trapped for hundreds of years.'

Eve nodded. She knelt down beside Amunnic's remains. Luke knelt beside her, holding the bowl sideways. 'I think this might be a situation where a credit card will actually work,' she said. She pulled her AmEx out of her purse and used it to scoop the ashes into the bowl.

When all that was left on the floor was a greasy scorch mark, Luke slid the bowl's lid in place. He started to stand, but Eve put her hand on his arm. 'I'm so glad you're OK.' Those words didn't come close to expressing how she felt, how relieved and just joyful she was that Luke was alive and by her side.

'I'm glad you're OK too,' he answered. He reached out and cupped her cheek with his hand. 'You're pretty awesome, you know that?'

Then they were kissing. With no thought, no awkwardness, no 'Is this really a good idea?'. Just perfection. Perfect perfection.

And no cat-demon to interrupt.

'Has Peter asked you anything about seeing me use my zap?' Eve asked Jess. They stood in front of the portal the next afternoon, waiting for Luke. They'd decided sending Amunnic's ashes back to hell was the safest way to deal with them.

Jess shook her head. 'I think he wants to forget the whole thing ever happened. He hasn't said anything about the demon either. Actually nobody said anything when we were all waiting to get picked up from the hospital, except Cathy, and she's pretty much convinced herself she had some fever hallucination. I think it helped that the puncture marks closed up right away.'

'Sorry I'm late,' Luke called as he hurried over to them. 'My dad wanted to go out to lunch. Recovering from the plague has given him an insane appetite.' Happiness radiated off Luke. Eve could feel it flowing into her. 'We ran into Mr Dokey,' he added. 'I never thought I'd see him alive, but he was wolfing down pizza at Piscatelli's. It's freaky how good he looks. It's like his skin regenerated itself. It still looks a little grey and he's definitely skinnier, but that's it.'

'I'm appreciating the skills of that priest who put the curse on Amunnic more and more,' Jess said, rubbing the spot on her hand where the necrosis had been. 'It's amazing how all the symptoms of the plague disappeared. I'm a little tired, but that's all.'

'Not too tired to go out with Seth tonight,' Eve teased.

'Never,' Jess answered.

'I knew he'd understand why you freaked when you first saw him with the necrosis,' Luke commented.

'He more than understood. He actually apologized for looking so repulsive,' Jess exclaimed.

'I'm having to do that all the time – and I didn't even get the plague,' Luke joked. His expression turned serious as he took the bowl out of his backpack. He'd kept it in the church overnight. Eve and Luke had agreed that was the safest place.

'I'm not sure how to open the portal,' Eve said. 'I guess I'll just experiment. And hope that nothing is crouched on the other side waiting to come out.'

'I've got my *hi-yah* ready,' Jess assured her.

'And I have the sword.' Luke tapped his back. 'Just in case.'

'Then we're all good. Nothing will get by the Trio of Terror,' Eve said. She knelt down in front of the arch and touched the opening with the fingertips of both hands. The golden tapestry appeared, sparkling and glinting in the mild March sunlight.

*It's made of energy*, she thought. And she could absorb energy. She'd learned that.

Eve opened herself to the energy of the tapestry and felt the power at her core brighten with the infusion. She didn't want to destroy the block, just make a little hole. She moved her hands lightly over a section at the bottom of the tapestry, until the threads in that piece loosened, became translucent, and disappeared. Eve heard a soft sucking sound from the other side that made her mouth taste metallic. 'It should go through now,' she said, without lifting her hands away.

Luke knelt beside her and pushed the bowl containing Amunnic's ashes through the portal. It hovered for a moment, then began to fall, disappearing as it did.

As soon as she saw the bowl vanish, Eve released power through her fingertips, the golden waves repairing the tapestry. The hole closed in moments, but Eve kept sending her power out, enjoying the warm surge, urging more threads to form, creating another layer of protection over the portal's opening, another layer between the demons who lived on the other side and all the people she loved on this one.

It wasn't until she heard a soft cough behind – one that hadn't sounded like it came from Luke or Jess – that she pulled her hands away. She stood and turned, anxious about her power being observed.

Callum and Alanna stood a few metres away, their expressions solemn. *Why was the Order here?* Eve walked over to them, Jess and Luke on either side of her. In spite of her surprise, she realized there was a question that she wanted an answer to. Maybe the Order would know . . .

'So many people from so many places could have bought that bowl at the marketplace in Egypt,' Eve said to Callum. 'It can't be a coincidence it ended up in Deepdene, can it?'

The lines around his mouth deepened as he prepared to answer. 'Even with the portal closed, Deepdene will attract darkness.'

'Demons, you mean,' Eve said.

'Yes,' Callum said simply. 'Although the door is closed at this moment, they can sense it has been opened recently. Lord Medway created something that can never be completely destroyed when he made the portal.'

'So we can expect more, even with the portal blocked?' Luke asked.

'It's possible,' Callum answered, and Eve felt a knot of apprehension form in her belly.

'*Very* possible,' Alanna added. She glanced at Callum, as though waiting for him to say something more.

'Did you come for a kind of final report on Amunnic?' Eve asked when Callum remained silent, studying her with his shrewd grey eyes.

'I emailed you guys all the details,' Luke said. Eve noted that he didn't seem particularly pleased to see Alanna.

'Did it feel the same as when you've killed other demons with your power?' Callum asked Eve.

She shrugged. 'Pretty much. It didn't feel like it took quite as much power as killing Malphas, but I had my hands right on Amunnic. Maybe that made a difference.'

'Was he able to bite you?' Alanna asked, and Eve thought she asked the question with way too much eagerness. Like she wanted Eve to say yes and give her all the gory details.

'No,' she answered. Callum raised an eyebrow. 'He did scratch me though. More than scratch, really. He dug that claw of his right into my neck.'

'Drawing blood?' Alanna asked, with that same strange eagerness.

'Yeah. I could feel it running down,' Eve told her.

'We believe that is what killed the demon.' Callum hesitated. 'That may be why you felt that you had to use less power. Your blood is poisonous to Amunnic.'

'What?' Jess burst out. 'That makes no sense. Human blood can't be poisonous to Amunnic, surely. He lives on it.'

'Eve, remember we took a sample of your blood the last time we were here?' Callum asked her.

'You said testing it might help you come up with more ways to kill demons, since I can kill them without one of the special swords,' Eve replied. 'Is that what you found out? That my blood is poisonous to demons because I'm the Deepdene Witch?'

'We found a reference in our archives. The only thing Amunnic is unable to survive is exposure to the blood of another demon,' Callum said. Usually his gaze was strong and direct, but he dropped his eyes for a moment.

Luke frowned. 'What does that have to do with Eve's blood though?'

The knot of anxiety in Eve's stomach grew larger and harder. She suddenly didn't want to hear what Callum would say next, especially when he looked her in the face again and she saw a mix of revulsion and pity in his eyes.

'We got the results of the tests on your blood back,' Callum told her. He hesitated.

Alanna shot a pointed look at Luke, then said, 'Eve, the results revealed that you have demon blood.'

# Look out for the next
# Dark Touch story

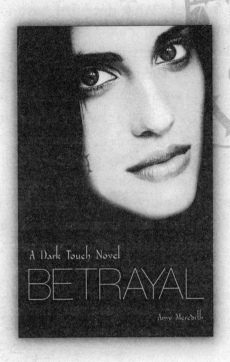

A Dark Touch Novel

BETRAYAL

Amy Meredith

Eve is starting to love her role as the
Deepdene Witch. She and Luke are finally
a couple, Jess is off to prom — things
are looking up . . .

But not for long.

Weird sightings of dead animals
around town immediately set off alarm
bells for Eve, Jess and Luke. Then the
demons start appearing . . .

# Fall under the spell of Dark Touch . . .

## Available now

# HAVE YOU EVER FALLEN IN LOVE?

978 0 552 50173 0

978 0 385 61809 0

Discover the series that the
whole world is talking about.

**'Dark and romantic, an absolute
blinder of a book'** *The Sun*

By Lauren Kate

# A glamorous slice of vampire life
## – with a sinister edge …

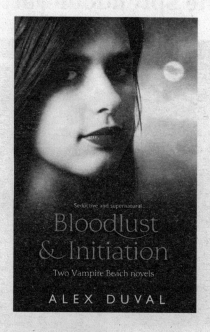

Jason has just moved to Malibu – home to rich kids and fabulous parties. He's flattered to be included – and very flattered by the interest of the stunning Sienna. But Sienna and her friends hide a dark secret … and Jason is risking his life by falling for her.

Two Vampire Beach novels in one.

**'Outrageously addictive, super cool …'**
*The Bookseller*

978 1 862 30896 1